Love Spirits

What Happens in Venice:

Book One

DIANA CACHEY

ISBN: 1481031767
ISBN 13: 9781481031769
Library of Congress Control Number: 2014906966
CreateSpace Independent Publishing Platform
North Charleston, South Carolina

This is a work of fiction. All of the characters, organizations, and events
portrayed in this novel are either products of the author's
imagination or are used fictitiously.

This Book is Dedicated to
My Husband, Joseph Cachey III

CONTENTS

Dear wide-eyed tourist,

Don't go to Venice.

But if you do, don't fall in -- in a canal, in love or into Venice itself. As if you have a choice. Hear us cackling?

Listen. We came to warn you about La Serenissima, the Most Serene One, as Venice has been called since before the Middle Ages. You will not heed our warning and you will come looking for us. How do we know? It happens every time a Venetian ghost story is told.

As ancient protectors of the Venetian republic, we ghosts guard her virtues of which she has many. One reason we love her, and you will too, is that she is stuck in time. Did you know Venice functions without motorcars or trucks? We don't like motorcars or trucks. Hundreds of tiny islands sewn together by foot bridges leaves no need for noisy, fume-spewing vehicles, thankfully.

We prefer floating.

Our classic transport is the gondola. Mostly reserved for you tourists now, gondolas are and always have been helmed by the most prestigious oarsmen in the world -- highly trained gondoliers who stand while rowing through the labyrinth of canals. They don't mind when we ride with or without you while they serenade us with opera, Frank Sinatra songs and romantic favorites.

Ah yes, romance. As one visitor put it, "It's their schtick, a Venetian ploy, an act to get sexy with you." It is true. Venice equals romance equals sex.

If the shadows of Venice frighten you or you feel like you're in a dream, have fun with it, float with us. We are watching over you. We want to further your journey to a more magical life because we think a person is charmed by a trip to La Serenissima.

It could change your soul forever. Just ignore this cautionary tale.

We remain in your service,
The Venetian Ghosts

UNO (1)

The Ghost Card

Venice kidnapped her. It stole her breath, it made her weep, and she forgave it. This trip was no different.

Palazzos flanked the Grand Canal as if playing the role of soldiers obedient to the eyes of tourists who passed in public boats, water taxis and gondolas. These old palaces sparkled on water like porcelain figurines on a glass shelf. A soft breeze rolled across Louisa's cheeks and it rippled the reflections and transformed the scene. Mesmerized by the magic, Louisa missed her boat stop.

No problem, she thought, *I'll find another place for coffee.* She refused to drink it alone in her apartment and religiously sipped her brew at one of the little cafes where handsome Venetian men worked. There were many such establishments on her way to police headquarters.

When she arrived a few weeks earlier, American lawyer Louisa Mangotti hoped to spearhead the creation of an essential link between Venice police and the rest of the world. But was she leading the department into the future of global law enforcement as she'd envisioned? No, she sat shackled to a desk where she sorted and translated police data because Interpol sent red alerts and formal requests for information in English or French, not in Italian. Therefore, many unsolved crimes remained ignored in the file drawers of the lagoon city, a thriving metropolis and huge tourist destination. And Louisa? Louisa remained bored in a cubicle learning about law and disorder.

According to recent updates to her sister, Louisa was focused on everything but international law enforcement anyway:

> *Ciao Barbara, Remember that lagoon island said to be full of ghosts where patients with the plague were once sent to die? Well many other haunted places exist in Venice too. I don't believe in ghosts, not like you do, but I am checking out some haunts. I am checking out Venetian men too.*

Because Barbara objected, Louisa promised not to explore the haunted island. But didn't Barbara object to Louisa going to Venice at all this time? Wasn't it just like Barbara to try to direct everything, even from afar? How much of the seemingly haunted happenings in Venice could Louisa ignore?

Blame the postcard, thought Louisa. And as she thought it, a loud bell rang out.

Louisa took note. In Italy, it is customary to pause and recall whatever you were thinking when a bell chimes, especially this bell, the one that echoed from the famous bell tower, high above St. Mark's Square. The massive San Marco bell continued to sound in the serene setting, *bang, gong, gong, bang,* and it reverberated across the *piazza,* across the lagoon, to the nearby islands of Murano and Lido. It sounded authoritative and mighty. Every day. For centuries.

What was I thinking about when the San Marco bell rang, wondered Louisa, *the postcard?*

Before she left for Venice, Louisa was tugging on the edges of papers jammed into her mail slot when a single postcard fell, one that pictured a gondola floating under the Bridge of Sighs. The card bore a Venetian postmark and was emblazoned with a red wax seal. Inked in elaborate calligraphy, it read: *Dear Louisa, Come to Venice but don't fall in. In a canal, in love or into Venice itself -- as if you have a choice. Listen, we need you and you are curious. See you soon, The Venetian Ghosts.* She'd read it many times, could recite it word-for-word. Like a mother, a lover, a provocateur, Venice had sent its special calling card.

Or did Matteo send that card?

Years ago, she and her then Venetian lover, Matteo, explored the mazes and alleys of Venice together, such that Louisa knew the town better than many locals who rarely ventured further than two bridges from their homes. She expected to see Matteo when she arrived in *Piazzale Roma,* the drop-off area where the bridge from the mainland stops, cars and buses meet their final end and visitors or inhabitants abruptly exchange the real world for a dreamland of cobblestone and concrete mazes, dark corners, dancing shadows and rows of houses that stop smack-dab at a canal, much to the dismay of unsuspecting wanderers.

The familiar whistle she'd heard the day she arrived wasn't from Matteo but from a porter loading luggage into a barge for delivery to her apartment. In the past, either Matteo hauled her bags or she dragged them herself. Those days were gone now and Louisa, an attorney and more of princess, paid the porter's price. She didn't need Matteo anymore. She stared off the back of the boat en route to her morning espresso. *Ah Matteo,* she sighed, recalling memories of him.

The San Marco bell rang again and a large hand tapped her shoulder. There he stood, Matteo, beside her in the open air smoking section of the ferry, as if alerted to her presence by the wind. Despite all she'd accomplished since she last saw him, Matteo's body next to hers changed her back into an insecure romantic, the younger girl who thought life with this tortured man was possible.

She watched him take the longest breath of air she'd ever seen a person take then pull a cigarette out of a pack. With villain written all over his handsome face, years after she fell in love with him, Matteo's dark green eyes lured her over his cigarette. He paused to light it. He moved into her. His physique filled any space between them. Yet below his thickly curled lashes, his eyes urged her even closer. With his uneven lips perched into a one-sided smile, he seemed to have aged in that charming way men age but, Louisa feared, women did not. Bundled in typical Venetian work clothes, a long parka with fur trim and a grey scarf wrapped carefully around his neck, he might as well have been naked. His hair was perfect.

She fought the impulse to kiss him and he took another one of those bottomless breaths, this time from the cigarette. He steadied it, relished his slow first drag of tobacco, exhaled, and instantly took another firm determined puff, such that anyone near him could see how much he enjoyed smoking, that it relaxed him. Louisa was not at all relaxed by the sight of Matteo and she wanted that cigarette for herself.

She never felt relaxed around Matteo, who engineered it that way. The insulting, selfish brute mixed with the witty, sensual charmer. *Years later, years too late, will I be forever drawn to this man, even though he makes me absolutely miserable?*

He felt it too, the heat between them, her indecision. In an instant, he moved position, stood flat up against her, pressed his body further into hers, right there in the boat.

Like he owns me. Like his body owns me. God, he smells good, thought Louisa, who couldn't stop the continued rise of warmth within her.

"Stop it," she said out loud, half to herself and half to Matteo's wandering eyes, while he ran one hand up and down her body and ran both eyes up and down the nearest tightly outfitted woman. With this sort of erratic behavior, Matteo destroyed their relationship years ago but somehow his torrid, Venetian magnetism always allured her. Her sister despised Matteo and referred to him as *that drop-dead gorgeous thug*. At the moment, Louisa had to agree with her sister's frustrating description of him.

To Barbara's relief, Louisa stayed away from Matteo for years while she went to law school. Never the loyal lover, Matteo pacified his rage over her absence with too much liquor and not enough women. To Louisa, her education meant freedom.

To Matteo, it meant war. Yet, she longed for him, wanted him to this day. *He's just a distraction*, thought Louisa.

The public boat, or *vaporetto,* approached its next stop. She twirled her hair and gazed at centuries-old buildings whose vibrant colors cast their ghosts onto the canal. The boat stopped, and she jumped from Matteo before he could put out the cigarette or remove his eyes from the buxom beauty near them.

Louisa flew up the aisle, out the open boat gate and off to find a little Venetian coffeehouse.

Too early for tourists barely awake for tours, not too early for Louisa, she savored the serene scene while Venice settled into its day. Within hours, the lovely Saint Mark Square would bustle with children, musicians, waiters, street artists, Italians, Germans, Brits, Frenchmen, Greeks and pigeons (pigeons being, appropriately, Venetian slang for tourists). The square was the meeting place for everybody who was anybody. All would mingle and gawk, eat and drink, snap and pose for photos and paintings. All would carry on in this fashion until well past nightfall, as they had done for centuries.

Did the ghosts haunt Saint Mark Square for centuries too? Louisa wondered. A church bell tolled. *Bells again*, she noted. She pulled out her ghost research and read:

> A member of the Barbaro family married the daughter of Giavanni Dario and bought the Palazzo Ca' Dario. Death plagued the owners of this sinister dwelling, known as the palace that kills.

Louisa envisioned the impressive and supposedly haunted Ca'Dario palace. Its arched windows and prominent location made it memorable to public boat passengers who regularly viewed it. *The Palace that kills,* thought Louisa. *How many people died there?* She read further:

> Many legends hover over Ca' Dario as do the ghosts of owners such as the Barbaros whose lives were lost or destroyed. Other deaths included suicides of English scholar, Rawdon Brown, and his friend, the homosexual lover of Charles Briggs, who killed himself after Briggs left hastily. Count Filippo Giardano's lover, Raul, bashed in the Count's skull with a statuette and manager of the rock band, The Who, also died violently there.

To Louisa, the gilded palace looked nothing like a haunted house, except perhaps for the moldy, cracked plaster created by centuries of flooding and fog, but then again, so were many Venetian houses. She didn't think she believed in ghosts. *But that Interpol job did seem to fall in my lap,* she thought. *Just like the ghost card.*

A light drizzle forced Louisa to suspend her reflections and tuck the notebook under her coat. She passed through *Campo San Maurizio* and found Cafe Redentore, one of her favorite places for morning brew. With a cold cheek pressed against the window, she peered inside and saw steam billow up from newly formed peaks of foamed milk. Decorated in typical Venetian cafe style, the cafe's wood-walls and dark-beamed ceilings reminded her of a sailboat kitchen. Brown and beige ceramic checkered tiles, green marbled counters and brick archways made the cafe quaint and welcoming. It was cozy, meaning tiny.

From inside the cafe, a waiter recognized Lousa's familiar face even with her thick cashmere scarf wrapped around it and waved her in.

"*Ciao Marino,*" said Louisa to the good-looking Venetian.

"*Come zea, tutto ben?*" How are you, asked the waiter in thick local dialect, already preparing her coffee, *doppio macchiatone,* or large double espresso with a dollop of steamed milk on top, as was her usual.

"*Beh, beh, anca ti?*" Very well, she answered back in dialect. She loved practicing her *Veneziano* and uproarious laughter followed whenever this blond American beauty tried to speak it. The routine had become part of their morning entertainment.

"*Si, si, anca mi,*" he answered that he was fine, too. Several other handsome men entered the cafe, all greeting Louisa with *ciao veccia*. Translated literally, it meant "hello old lady" but in the humorous and often vulgar Venetian dialect, it was a term of endearment meaning simply "dear old friend."

"*Ciao veccio,*" she said, pronouncing it perfectly, and adding to their laughter. In these little Venetian cafes, everybody knew Louisa. All of her mornings in Venice were uncomplicated and joyous like this one -- with no raging traffic commutes, no isolation inside her vehicle, no standing alone in line at a coffee shop where few knew her nor seemed to care. In this lagoon city, like a strange fishbowl, local and long-term visiting fishes watched out for others. A plethora of *buon giornos* and *ciao veccias* addressed her while the cafe filled with customers.

She downed her *macchiatone* standing at the counter, not only because Venetians charge more for table service, but because locals drank their coffee at the bar. As did she, like a local.

Why would I go back to America and leave all of this? she thought as she departed the cafe. The moon peeked at Louisa between buildings and reflected on the lagoon as she breezed through the symphony of Venice at dawn.

She often woke early or stayed up long enough to witness the city's unique arousal. She loved to watch, amused, as *"ping, pang, ping"* went the shutters when Venice wearily woke up. Boat throttles chugged, pigeons scattered, early workers trotted along the canals. Her eyes widened and the morning show built to its crescendo. Storefront slates slapped up, kiosks quickly stocked with goods. Foot and boat traffic increased, canals filled with all manner of water craft. A full-fledged water and street performance arrived after dawn's quiet overture.

Venice at dawn is wonderful, thought Louisa as she gingerly avoided puddles left by recent rain.

Puddle after puddle she trudged to St. Mark's Square, whose symphony had not yet started. In the square, she sat at an empty table carefully chained down for the night and leaned her head back to survey the tall bell tower. When she heard the bells chime earlier this morning, *no, not a chime, a loud gong,* she'd been reflecting on the ghosts. It made her think of the ghost walk she'd taken and stories the guide told, made more eerie by fog and drizzling rain. She shivered and, hoping to shake off the haunting chill, she began her morning Italian lesson while waiting for the San Marco cafe to open.

She started her Italian lesson by reading the local newspaper and a story about two recently drowned glassmakers turned her thoughts back to Matteo. His sister, Angelica, had married a glassblower from the same factory on Murano Island where the dead glassmakers worked. Angie at one time had even persuaded her husband to hire Matteo to train in the prestigious art of glassblowing. Glassmaking came easy to Matteo, of course, being gifted at most things. He fashioned glass pieces that normally took years of apprenticeship to learn to create. The factory's Maestro considered seniority a priority so he refused to promote Matteo based on talent. The Maestro did offer him overtime and weekend assistant jobs to help with quick advancement in the company but Matteo wasn't interested in "working that hard." He soon bitterly left their employ. Blessed with Venetian good looks and family money, Matteo didn't need the job. He always spoke disdainfully of glassmakers, and especially "that factory," after he left.

According to the newspaper, the police were considering these two drownings suspicious. Possible homicides.

"*Vuoi un altro,*" said a waiter dressed in white tuxedo, interrupting Louisa's musings about dead glassmakers and Matteo. He asked if she wanted another coffee, unaware that Louisa hadn't ordered one and had only occupied the empty table while waiting for the cafe to open.

"*Macchiatone, per favore,*" she said. She scribbled in her notebook: *Ask Matteo about Ca' Dario, the Barbaro family, my ghost card and these glassmakers.*

Another bell rang. *Bells again*, thought Louis. *Ca' Dario, its curse, ghost letter, glassmakers, all important*, she wrote and grabbed her purse. She pulled out the ghost card she'd

10

received in America and waved off the waiter, who hadn't moved to get her coffee but was instead peering over her shoulder at her notes.

She recalled that when she received the ghost card -- as she'd started to call the postcard signed by the Venetian ghosts -- a neighborhood cat cowered under her porch. His eyes had stayed peeled on the postcard she held in her hand until a strong wind blew it onto the sidewalk next to him. The dutiful predator pounced, paw outstretched, to block the card's retreat from her. "Thanks, Marco," she'd said to the cat in America, whom she'd nicknamed after the winged-lion of St. Mark, patron of Venice. When she reached for the card, Marco had lifted his paw but another gust blew it away. Quicker than the wind, Marco held it down with both paws this time until she retrieved it. "Strange, very strange," she'd said to Marco the cat. He seemed to understand her for he'd nodded his head. She recalled her snowy American yard and the vast driveway leading to a garage that held two fast cars.

Venice is slow, Venice has no cars, she had thought the day the ghost card arrived, and Marco the cat had nodded his head again in agreement.

Outside Seattle where she lived in America, meeting places were found after long drives in traffic. In Venice, every place, every inch of every walk was a potential meet and greet. Louisa noted that the meeting spot of preference for pigeons of both varieties was right in *Piazza San Marco*, where she now sipped her expresso. Awestruck faces began to flood into the no longer quiet spot.

She clutched the ghost card. Whoever sent it somehow knew that she'd go looking for him, her, them. No one, nothing, could keep her away from Venice this time. Truth be told, she'd fallen in. Again.

Louisa left the cafe and began to negotiate the mazes towards Rialto. She tried hard to concentrate more on the beautiful art of her surroundings and less on the seductive art of Matteo.

In the Venetian shadows, Matteo turned each corner behind her. Unnoticed.

❧

I hate funerals, that's why I didn't want one.

It is why my romance with Venice would never end and why no words were spoken during my final night there.

She took me out to the Grand Canal and the click of her heels competed only with the sound of water that sloshed on concrete foundations and the knock of oak poles that anchored the dock. The wide canal rose and fell, its dark drink swirled and caught reflections of light then cascaded down from buildings and sprinkled it around us in twinkling ripples.

We weren't there long.

A distasteful sculpture -- that of a large glass-encrusted skull -- leered from across the canal. To me, the skull's hollow eyes, clenched jaw and gnashing teeth presented an amusing backdrop, an appropriate set decoration. To her, the sculpture ruined the view and disturbed the reverence of our last moments together.

She turned from the skull and tossed my ashes into the canal where I floated and scattered like dead leaves on water.

William Shakespeare wrote that all the world is a stage but no stage compares to the beguiling city of Venice. With an open air theatre and constant flow of shows, Venetian dramas occur on canals, footpaths and bridges, or in bars, churches and public plazas. Life in Venice entertains and mesmerizes an interactive, impromptu audience. Scenes are acted out on water or next to it, like my farewell to life on the Grand Canal.

She watched my floating cremains disperse and disappear. Some men nearby watched too. They pondered her while she pondered me. This tragedy, this scene on a boat dock stage, it changed her fate. A curtain seemed to fall. She wept.

Although I yearned for one last stroke of her soft calves and tried to reach for her leg, she faded in the distance. Alone. I knew she would seek solace. Those men knew it too.

She spread my ashes in the Grand Canal with great resistance and only with greater insistence by me. I didn't tell her to stay in Venice but I hoped she would. Could she become part of the play, find those things she wanted, submerge into the city's ever-changing lights and sets?

I had plans for her. Venice had plans for her. She had other plans.

Yet, Venice -- moldy, dusty, touristy, wet, serene, sensual, antique -- had cast its spell on her the moment she exited the train station and scanned the splendid playground before her, that of the infamous Grand Canal. My current resting place.

Venice. Where the lines between old and new, east and west, life and death, humor and horror, sand and glass, water and land vanish, so did I.

Until now . . .

☙❦❧

DUE (2)

Ⱨer Ȿiȿter'ȿ Ⱪeeper

Barbara trudged a peaceful path in the rough Seattle winter. Even with a blistered left instep incessantly rubbing against her shoe, she smiled at the scene. A rare snow surrounded her, filled parking spaces, blanketed yards with fluffy piles and lined the lonely lanes. Sparkling flakes fell among birch trees now barren of leaves that reached out their silhouetted branches coated with ice. Against the white backdrop, hundreds of Christmas bulbs not yet put away reflected brighter light.

Ah fresh air, fresh snow, she thought, *if only it would inspire fresh ideas.*

The canopies of trees and lovely breeze did not inspire ideas or answers. *Damn that Louisa, why doesn't she come home?* For the first time in years, Louisa had left for Venice alone. When Louisa studied there in college, Barbara often visited, enjoying Carnival parties, famed regattas, spring breaks and summer beaches. Barbara wondered why her sister hadn't invited her to visit this time.

She thought for a moment. Louisa's latest email said she'd found no respite within her apartment's drafty, concrete walls:

> *Dear Barbara, Lucky you're not here. Venice is colder, windier, fiercer than usual. Brrrr. I've blocked all the windows with pillows and wear three layers inside my house. Four or five layers, if I go out, which I must do because it is Venice, right? Bundled up and useless as fashion goes. But look at the attached picture of a Venetian girl, all perfect in this weather! Fur hat, scarf, thigh high boots squeezed into tight jeans and jacket cinched at the waist by a leather belt to emphasize her hour-glass figure, which is totally uncalled for. She probably struts the campo like that to piss everyone off. It worked. I hate her.*

Nope, not an invitation. More a dissuader. Still, Louisa was feeling the strains of competition from Venetian beauties on their home turf. She was also freezing and miserable. Weather and perfectly dressed Italians aside, something else Louisa had mentioned kept Barbara awake at night:

> *Don't freak but Matteo could take me to the island of ghosts. Yes, I said Matteo.*

How could Barbara not freak out? Matteo, the wolf, that deviant disturbed her more than any haunted island. He'd ensnare Louisa in more of his drama. Barbara's concern was not that Louisa couldn't handle Matteo, it was that she would try.

What is wrong with that girl? Normal women don't leave home, move to Venice and hook up with hoodlums at the drop of a postcard, do they?

Barbara knew from experience that an addiction to beguiling Venice was harmless compared to Louisa's addiction to Matteo. Despite trying not to judge, judgments filled Barbara and she blamed all her frustration on Louisa, whose selfish actions--of going to Venice without her and staying too long -- were the cause of all this worry. Barbara began to mentally arrest, convict and sentence Louisa. Her crime? Having too much fun and time in Venice, with and without Matteo. Her sentence? To return from Venice immediately.

What do I do? Barbara asked the cold air about her, or was it God from whom she sought guidance?

From time to time, as she did now, she asked someone, something outside of her, for help. It seemed to answer when she needed it most. Although some called it intuition, others called it crazy. This time, the answer made her feel queasy for the air chanted a response. It made no sense:

Clouds have passed, the leaves have turned, the passing stage, the turning world. May the thoughts fill you with the words to say and then shall you say them to those Venetian ghosts . . .

Ghosts. When Louisa's surprising and alluring job offer came from the Venice police *commissario*, Barbara thought it all too suspect. Then Louisa left in extreme haste after receiving a card allegedly from Venetian ghosts.

More likely from Matteo, noted Barbara.

Louisa had told her of a small society of ghosts, which Venetians alleged would walk the alleys and ride in gondolas. They moved amongst the living and achieved more "form" everyday. The ghosts loved Venice, had been there a thousand years and considered themselves keepers of the city, watchdogs of a mysterious sort. The many mask shops offered them seclusion, a place where they could slip behind a mask or cloak and hide in plain sight. Empty, hollow apartments offered shelter or a place to host their haunted parties, in as grand a style as any Venetian was want to do. In traditional dress, the ghosts hid, watched people and found ways to protect them. These so-called ghosts had planted clues for Louisa, clues that were secretive or vague--a haunted Murano house, Nazi connections and a cursed palace that kills.

Take charge of the situation? Do what I do best? Control things.

Barbara needed to see, touch, feel what was going on there in Venice and then bring Louisa back. How? She'd already failed to influence Louisa many times, like when she tried to persuade Louisa not to got to Venice at all.

She'd even taken Louisa for an alternative taste of Italy in a little bistro before she left. She'd thought the ploy was working when they spied two fashionably dressed, handsome men at the restaurant that day. One man wore a hooded soft wool sweatshirt adorned with the word Italia in navy letters. The other boasted his taut chest in a tight shiny black T-shirt. Barbara whispered to Louisa, "I think they're Italian."

Together the sisters ogled the tallest of the two men, his spiked black hair held dutifully in place with gel, brown suede Gucci sneakers peaked out from under the hem of carefully torn jeans that rounded out his rump. They next surmised his friend, whose attire highlighted his fit anatomy with impeccable tailoring and whose white-soled black leather loafers finished off the polished look.

"Gorgeous and dressed in designer threads," said Louisa that day, "but not Italian and they like each other, not us." Barbara turned to see that the man in the tight black tee had wrapped his hand around the thigh of the hooded one.

This gesture, this touch of a man by another man, would mean nothing in Italy, where public affection between men was strangely commonplace in an otherwise machismo world. Italian men touched men. They were affectionate with cousins, soccer mates, neighbors and, with the proper introduction, other men they may have just met. All touching, even touching another man, is encouraged by men in Italy.

Not so in Seattle. Here, this caressing of another man's leg confirmed that their sexual orientation was the source of their fashionista perfection, not an Italian heritage. Louisa had then toasted Barbara with a cock of the head and said, "Italian men are waiting for me out there," and she pointed off, out into some faraway land.

Barbara's reply had been cocky too. "So that is your sexcuse for going to Venice," she'd said.

"My sexcuse?" said Louisa, head no longer cocked but twisted. "Is it a sexcuse or a dream assignment in our favorite place on earth?" She'd said it calmly but Barbara knew she had succeeded in baiting her sister. "Anyway, who cares? I may end up doing nothing but searching for ghosts and eating pasta, pizza and pastries," Louisa added.

"As well as also drinking copious amounts of espresso, wine and grappa," Barbara said.

"My trip will be more like a memoir called *One Woman's Loss of Her Virginity and Other Lies About Italy,*" said Louisa. She also thought, *you might want to miss this trip.*

They both laughed but Barbara wasn't laughing anymore. Stuck here in Seattle, bemoaning Louisa's fate, she didn't want to miss this trip. She'd left her lagoon town, the place that stole her heart the minute she saw it. Long ago, or so it seemed, she'd vanished from Venice.

She tried to focus on something else. She stopped and forced herself to look about, to breathe the air. She was back in the now and she saw branches thrusting onto roof edges, birds perched up on hedges and the sun shining on fresh snow. Across this pale expanse, students filed to school, seemingly full of wisdom with piles of books. She felt ambitious watching them and feelings began to violently dance around her, inside her. Then she heard it.

Those poetic, haunting words, which of late had whispered to her during her walks:

> *Calm in the evening, quick in the morn, days end here as they dawn. Curtains drop or raise, lovers come and go, within the master's framework, the waters of life flow. Neglected at the onset, savored when it's gone. Her knowledge grows thick and taut with every rook and pawn. In lures unknown to foreign shores, they frolic and jump. Sad eyes lost, tossed in nets, killing the smallest and the poor.*

What did they mean? These words? Words she'd first heard the day Louisa left for Venice. Although she'd traversed this lonely stretch many times before, she never heard voices. Let alone poetry. Since Louisa went to Venice this time, Barbara heard, or sensed, the same words every time she walked this part of her route.

"In lures unknown to foreign shores. Sad eyes lost. In nets," she repeated out loud.

Nets? Fish or shrimp nets, she wondered as she pictured the vast wetlands surrounding the Venetian lagoon. Were these poems from beyond the grave? From a ghost?

Interesting, she thought. *Should I be writing these all down?*

As if it weren't all silly enough--this talk of masked, caped or costumed ghosts and whispered poetry on her peaceful walk--Barbara also suspected a Venetian that Louisa said she recently met might not be a man, but a ghost.

She had to get to Venice, to Louisa. In the meantime, something told her she should do what she always did when flustered or unsure--Barbara would sit on a cushion and meditate. She headed home with every intent to do so.

೯⊙൬

There, on the cushion, she relaxed, allowed her emotions to flow. Something didn't click. Something was hidden. Not of this world or time? "Bring me to the answers," she whispered. She concentrated on her breathing but bursts of thought peaked through cloudy breath.

Showing Louisa books. Methods. Research. Increased abilities. Stay away from that stuff, they said.

Barbara inhaled, exhaled and opened her eyes to return to the now with a soft gaze.

A brass rocking horse, a candelabra, a Buddha. Silk oriental scarfs, Indian pillows, homemade quilts with scraps from clothes mom made me as a child, but mom didn't make the quilt. She left. That's why Louisa ...

She closed her eyes but could still visualize her meditation room.

Embroidered flowers from the garden museum in London, a woman and a unicorn tapestry, a sheer hand painted skirt made into a curtain, prayer flags, his picture. Him. Could it be him? No, stop thinking of him. He left. Really left. Don't go there now.

Her eyes flew open again. She saw a Syrian drum, a steel drum, a chest painted with moon and stars. Zen tarot cards. She blinked her eyes and began breathing slow and deep.

Tarot. Supernatural beings. Spirits. Magnetic fields of ghosts whom she began to see as a child. "That's right, I see dead people," she told people who asked. "I've seen them all of my life."

Barbara surrendered to this train of thought, she let her mind go there. One of those dead people haunted her childhood home. Terrified when she first saw the thin elderly man in the basement, she fled up the stairs. He didn't follow her, never bothered her and seemed not to notice when she was present, so she got used to his shadowy presence. She decided that this ghost lived under the bench on the far wall because she mostly saw him near it. She also use to see him outside, just by the basement window near that space.

The ghost was a distinguished-looking man who wore a neat grey suit and carried a leather folder tucked under his arm. He searched about for things and took a final look around before he rushed off somewhere, fast. Late, he always seemed late. Nervous. At the same time, he seemed confident, proud.

Many days she saw him standing with his head held high facing the wall, lips moving. He seemed to punctuated his words with hand movements, pacing and changing his facial gestures into a scowl then a grimace or look of disgust. Then he'd start again, stopping at points to practice something over and over. He'd try it different ways and end with a pound of his fist on an imaginary table. He would hold his arms out as if talking to a group of people and it seemed he wanted them to agree with him because he scanned an imaginary group as if to make eye contact with individuals in rows then shook his head up and down slowly for each one. He would finally walk off, with a flourish. She saw him perform this routine several times. Seemingly the same speech or story to an imaginary panel. As if he needed to insure attention to his every word, silently he'd repeat and perfect as he went along. *Big thoughts.*

She concentrated on her breath but her mind drifted further, straying from the cushion into a vivid picture of the spirit in her basement.

After her father tore out the bench by the basement wall and installed a fireplace, she didn't see the elderly man's ghost again. When Barbara learned that a great trial lawyer once lived in the house, she felt sure it was his spirit who appeared there and the fireplace disturbed the energy and released him forever. Maybe the remodeled basement, now with a fireplace, became too hot for the attorney to bear?

Let's be clear here, I don't usually see full out walking, talking versions of dead people like when I saw him. Mostly they are shadows. Or whispers, she told herself.

A soft gong sounded, indicating her half hour meditation time was over. It hadn't gone well. *Whispers?*

Her mind was tired, her legs fell asleep, she was sick of thinking about stuff, stuff that wasn't working in her life. Lately she'd thought about making a change but panicked and did nothing. With no lover, with a job she no longer loved, she didn't exactly bounce out of bed ready to meet the day. Every new day was propelled by the tired inertia of the last.

"Go to Venice," whispered Barbara aloud to no one. In her cold meditation room, in the dead of winter, she nodded back her consent.

Flights, hotels, apartments. Clothes, jewelry, shoes. Check, check, check. She'd tried on sweaters, jeans, jackets, surveyed each item to determine the most Italian look and picked only the most flattering combinations. She lined up toiletries, stockings, scarves, lingerie and make-up, but not too much, she'd buy better stuff in Italy. Cat sitters were called to assess availability and suitability. Processed food was sneered at in grocery stores for savoring of fresh Venetian produce. The voluntary time-off she scoffed at months earlier when offered it, turned out to be a perk, not a temporary discharge due to shortage of work.

For Barbara, getting to Venice was easy. Finding ghosts in Venice? Harder. Fetching Louisa and releasing Matteo's grip?

Impossibile.

Louisa would scheme and stick until everyone else became unglued. If ghosts were to be found, Louisa would find them. Barbara hadn't stopped Louisa from going to

Venice so how would she get her home? Investigate the ghosts, disprove their existence?

Barbara imagined her own escape into those Venetian palaces, their moldy facades toppling into canals. Those quiet evenings with no traffic, strolling along sea water, visiting quaint bars or vegetable markets that hugged tiny bridges. Foggy thoughts of Venice led Barbara to recall how Louisa had written her about a fall, not into the arms of Matteo, but into a canal. She'd slipped on the algae-coated steps leading into a *traghetto* that ferries passengers across the Grand Canal and the only gondolas still in regular use by Venetians. This *traghetto* was her daily ride to work, so exposed algae didn't concern her. Yet, one day she'd been unable to maintain her balance long enough to avoid the dive. She'd fallen into the drink, straight out of the helpful hand of the gondolier, with her expensive Italian boots, cell phone and all.

"Venetians rallied so fast," she'd written to Barbara. "that my shoulders barely touched the water when they lifted me out of the canal as easily as a floating plastic bag." Her Venetian rescuers assured Louisa that all self-respecting residents fell into canals at some point in their lives. She'd been baptized, Venetian-style.

The young gondolier, feeling somewhat responsible for not holding her securely enough, made up for it by embracing her tightly. With both arms, he enveloped Louisa in his goose down parka and rubbed her wet body vigorously and lovingly.

Barbara smiled as she sensed Louisa's presence deep in her heart, thousands of miles across *the pond*--as was the Atlantic Ocean referred to by jet-setters like Louisa.

Don't fall in again, dear one, Barbara quietly prayed, *until I get there.*

She tried sending those words to Louisa, knowing not whether they fell onto her sister's distant ears.

TRE (3)

Prada

The San Marco bell towered behind Louisa during the brief walk to Rialto. With enough time for memories of Matteo to distract her, she almost missed the cafe, another cafe, the one where the medical examiner had asked her to meet him.

Where is this place anyway?

As usual in Venice, the minute she asked herself this, she was no longer lost and was standing in front of it. She smelled it. The sweet aroma of freshly baked croissants drifted out of the cafe and mingled with the pungent aroma of strong coffee. Inside, she ordered *brioche,* as they called croissants in Venice, then glanced around the room.

Prada. The single most alluring thing about him. A small red label on a grey ribbed knit wool hat. A design label that caused her to listen more closely to the sound of his soft, melodic voice. Especially the sweetness in it and the harmonic words he used.

Compelled to look closer at him, she eyed his blue wool sweater, obviously expensive and nicely finished, with a silk shirt collar standing up underneath it around his neck. *From wealth*, concluded Louisa. *Nothing wrong with that.*

Indeed everything was right about that. Wasn't it always right, when a man had money? This man with money stood casually confident with half-grown beard, dark curly hair and pale blue eyes. Wearing Prada.

"Nice," she mumbled softly. Nonetheless she was heard by others nearby, which was fine because if you want an Italian to admire you, you make it obvious that you admired him first. You stare directly at him, being certain to make eye contact. Then, when he sees you staring, you hold the stare. In Venice, the stare produced instant results. Instant sex in a bottle.

She didn't have time for sex. She didn't stare. She avoided eye contact. Still he magnetized her with some peculiar pull. Strong sensations flowed from him. She could see it. She saw flecks of gold between them. He saw it too, she noticed him look at the flecks then shake his head. As he shook, the gold burst apart and his pull relaxed from her.

She considered moving away from the Prada man and closer to the fire, more to see if he would follow than to elude him. She moved, he followed.

Ah, the wonderful ease of snagging a man in Venice, thought Louisa when the handsome stranger did indeed lean towards her.

However, her accumulated confidence shattered and was destroyed by his first words to her, "I knew you were American."

These harsh words spoken in English from the mouth of this pretty Prada boy crushed her. How did he know for sure she was American? Louisa possessed the striking features, the deep-set green eyes, full-lips and necessary bump on the nose, of her Italian heritage. She'd also dressed to emphasize her Mediterranean curves and head to toe in designer threads--that is, the latest fashion, not "last year American" as her Venetian friend had described Louisa's style when she arrived in Venice. To be sure, Louisa wore an ensemble that her Venetian gal pal had approved, when she dragged her into the nearest boutique to re-outfit her suitably in tight, somewhat revealing and expensive clothes. In the shop that day, her fashion-police friend had even looked at Louisa and said, "Who is dis woman? Everyone is staring at you. *Sono gelosa,* (I am jealous.)" Louisa herself had done a double-take and thought, *oh I wish I could look like that, beautifully Italian,* before realizing she was looking at her own made-over reflection.

For the man wearing Prada to say she looked American, well, it made her cringe.

Seeing her expression prompted him to correct himself. "Excuse my English. I think that was not correct. I mean to say *I knew you were American who I am to meet here today.*" As he explained this, he again left out the word "the" because he could not properly pronounce the sound of an English *th,* a sound not found in the Italian language. Probably the reason he hadn't used it the first time.

Louisa had forgiven him and thought, *oh I'm definitely the American you are supposed to meet today, you rich, sexy Venetian.* She almost said it out loud too. Instead, she laughed and offered her hand, hoping the attraction was mutual.

"I'm Louisa. Mangotti. An Italian surname, but I'm American," she said. "Thank you for agreeing to meet with me."

"Massimo Ricco," he said and nodded as they shook hands. His hands. So soft, so strong, so lingering. She couldn't help but see a gleam in his eyes during his brief scan of her figure.

In such a manner as to infer that his scan of her figure was to what she was responding, she said, "I see that you are Italian."

"Venetian," he corrected. Meaning not just another Italian or even one from another northern city -- for it was common knowledge that Northern Italians sometimes thought they were superior to other Italians, you know, like ones from the South. No, not an Italian nor a northerner, but a Venetian, superior to all other Italians. Superior for at least hundreds of years due to Venice's position, power, wealth, beauty and, as the once great republic, its status as the most powerful merchant state in the world. As if sensing that she was on the right track in deciphering his meaning, he said, *"Venezia e piu bella, no?"*

"Si," agreed Louisa, for she, like many people including Italians, thought Venice was the most beautiful city, one whose mystique goes back ages, inspiring poets, composers, painters. A museum itself, the city seems to topple into a lagoon as it rises from marsh. It is filled with ornate palaces, priceless paintings, hand-blown glass, carved furniture. It is embellished with angels, gargoyles, birds, crucifixes, flowers and saints, festooned with endless bas-reliefs and gilded-mosaics. Venice's unrivaled beauty then ripples out in endless reflections upon water, which heightens its appeal and distinguishes it from other great cities.

"I was born here," he added, meaning better than other inhabitants, ones who were not bred and born in Venice. She remembered Matteo often said of Venetian blood, "It is the top." Matteo, of course, being also pure Venetian.

Ah Matteo. In the way that Matteo was rough, bad, deceptive, Massimo was clean, pristine, true. Equally sexy, equally Venetian.

"I hope you understand, it is not possible to give you information of deaths. You ask me on phone," said Massimo. He then seemed to stumble for an English word, but finally said, "Of our investigation."

What Louisa heard him say and saw in his eyes was "I find you very attractive and you find me attractive too. Let's give each other an excuse to meet again. To discuss our investigation."

"Oh I see," she replied in such a manner as he could guess what she really heard him say and that she was agreeable to whatever he wanted. He didn't try to hide his interest in how provocatively she spoke those three words.

"Oh you see," he said in the same provocative way. "You are a lawyer and you're helping out our department with the Interpol translations and other matters and you understand? Of course, you do."

Yet, Massimo knew Louisa didn't understand at all. Not one bit. Despite an overwhelming attraction to her, he would need to be very careful with this one, clever and inquisitive. Any hint that he didn't want her snooping around would fuel her curiosity about the case, about him. He knew she liked what she saw of him, his physique, his style, his chiseled Venetian good looks.

But she didn't understand. She didn't know the real Massimo.

That morning at his private estate on the barely inhabited island of Vignole, Massimo had meticulously pieced together his latest picture, glueing seeds, creating detailed scenes. At age five, he developed a unique and sometimes bizarre fascination, a strange hobby of roaming the fields and gardens behind his grandfather's house on Vignole to look for seeds, to create pictures he knew he could never show to anyone. Massimo planted and plucked vegetables and flowers but he always picked and spilled their fresh seeds into sacks for his projects. By age fourteen he had amassed thousands of such pictures, his seed pictures, which collected dust in his tiny boathouse, which no one else could find. Mostly the pictures showed sadness and death and sex.

Massimo's obsession with death began after his parents and grandmother died in an alleged boating accident. Only his grandfather, his *nonno*, remained alive to comfort him. In his own grief-stricken life, papa Vito never asked why Massimo picked the seeds nor did he seem to care that the young boy spent so many hours in the remote boat shed.

Ten years after the death of his parents and grandmother, his dear Vito washed up on a trash-strewn beach on Vignole Island. The police department declared Vito's death an accidental drowning. Massimo never accepted it, nor any of these four deaths, as accidents. For his father and grandfather, like all Venetians, were skilled sailors, rowers, and swimmers who would not drown or wreck a boat. He resented and suspected the police involved in the investigation, who knew well the skill with which any member of his family could captain a boat, large or small. The conspiracy of silence won again.

Then Massimo inherited the family estate from his *nonno* at age fifteen and it negated the need for Massimo to ever have to work, for the rest of his life. It left him wealthy beyond all measure, even for a long-standing Venetian family like his, but it also left him with no other purpose and no one left to comfort him in his grief and anger. His isolation complete, he compulsively picked more seeds, glued them together, created mosaics, as he called them, which grew darker and more grotesque.

His obsession with death began with the loss of his parents and his grandmother, his *nonna*. It festered with the demise of his *nonno*. It fueled other obsessions. Creating seed pictures had much in common with dissection. To his great satisfaction, at age sixteen, he was accepted into a prestigious Italian university, where he received an advanced degree in Anatomy. He remained alone with his fears and science. Live humans long ago lost their appeal as did companionship and love. After he studied medicine and law, he became driven by the need to find justice for those who could only speak through their corpses. Holding a still hand, tweezing small areas and gluing and stitching others proved valuable in a current career as *medico legale*. He dissected these silent victims with the utmost care and respect, searching for answers where no one else could or would look. For he knew something about the criminals, the obsessed ones, that very few knew or would ever know. He knew what drove them.

"What can you tell me about the deaths of the glassmakers, *Dottore*?" Louisa asked, seeing something distant in his eyes, something dark.

"Not too much," he said blandly, "no more than you read in the paper and you can read Italian, Dottoressa Mangotti," he stated, not asking.

"I'm learning to read more Italian, yes, and call me Louisa," she said but pride in her title and language skills bubbled up.

"Louisa. I know you are working with our department in the translation and organization of data for the international crime agencies. It is the only reason I agreed to meet with you. Yes, I know you not only read Italian but speak it fluently and that you know Venetian as well," he said. He tried to say it in a formal tone but Louisa could see in his eyes that the thought of an American blonde speaking Venetian turned him on. "Now, you are intelligent and maybe trying to be help to us so I will tell you this, we are working on this case and it involves you not."

He was no longer interested in her sexually and hid something that even his sex-drive wouldn't allow to surface. *Until now,* Louisa decided.

"I don't think so," Massimo said, which interrupted her thoughts and she wondered if he was reading them.

"Dottore," she began.

"Please call me Massimo," he said as he bowed his head.

"Massimo. I think you will find it does involve me although it may not appear that way to you now."

"Splain me," he said. He mispronounced the word *explain*. His head tilted, not understanding the paradoxical statement Louisa had made.

Louisa had come to learn that paradoxes, satire and jokes often got lost in translation. She'd also come to learn that language ambiguities could be used to an advantage.

"I will explain it to you," Louisa promised, "but not today." Although she knew very little about the victims or their deaths, she planned to get more information in her usual determined way. Soon. From Matteo or his friends or both. Or from anyone she could persuade to reveal it.

She looked up and saw the half-smile on Massimo's face, almost as if he were giving her the go ahead in her plans to question Matteo and others about the case.

"When you bring information to me about these deaths," he said, "then I will bring information to you. Not before." Those were the same words that Louisa had planned to say to him next.

Louisa became all business-like in stiff body language but managed to flirt with her eyes. "Fair enough," she said and she handed him her business card. She turned to leave before he could beat her to that too. *Damn, I'm good,* she thought as she departed.

"Not as good as me," she thought she heard him say but she saw that his mouth was full, drinking coffee, when she heard it.

༄☙༄

Outside the bar, she saw Matteo huddled near the window, waiting.

"You're following me?" Louisa asked. "How did you get here? How did you find me?" She picked up her pace. More than the jealous-type, he could be violent.

"I'm Venetian. We know everything," he replied. He put a cigarette in his mouth, lit it, took a long puff then blew smoke at her in a sensual, almost coy, way.

34

"Oh you know? Everywhere I go?" she said although she believed it was true. Venetians watched out windows onto canals, *campos* and streets. They knew the bars each other frequented, the people each associated with and seemed to appear like mist in the maze-like city to magically find you around odd corners.

He nodded affirmatively, more like he was gracing her with a new truth than agreeing with her. "We see you when you don't see us."

"That may be true but I am not in Venice for you, Matteo." she said. "I have moved on from our, our..."

"Our what? Our love?"

"Yes," she said. Then she shook her head. "No. Not our love. Our affair."

"No, my darling, it is not possible to leave our love," he said. He pronounced it *loave* and drug out the word. He raised his chin and turned his long neck to her, his neck, tanned even in the winter from riding in boats and being outside. It looked as if he were presenting his neck to her. To kiss.

And kiss. And kiss. Louisa body shook. She tried to hide it and gasped for air.

His body shook and his lungs grabbed for air too. He met her eyes and didn't try to hide his own breathlessness or to apologize for it. Instead he perched his lips and gazed at her figure, then moved in and devoured her lips with his own. They both sighed as blood pumped through their loins and flushed their faces. Just like that, they both saw it, the fantasy. A frenzy of passion, not in bed or on a boat, but right there on the curb.

She tried to leave, but he stepped in her way. "What were you doing with, that, that," he paused as if looking for an unflattering word or could even end the sentence right there. "That man," he finally said in a brash tone. He grabbed her neck from behind, pulled her close and pressed his lips on her ear. "You," he paused again this time for emphasis, "are a candle in the wind."

With a wave of his head, he pulled away but didn't walk away. He stayed close, close enough for them to feel the heat of each other's bodies, even on a cold winter day. He looked as if he wanted to take her, right there. And he would make it wonderful, and she would let him.

To torture me, thought Louisa as she bit her lip.

"What do you want . . . me to say?" she said, as ambiguous as she could make her English.

"I don't understand you," he sneered.

"You don't understand me or my question?"

"I don't understand nah-ting," he said then thought better. "No, *you* don't understand nah-ting."

This time he didn't just stand there. He gripped her around the waist, fingers clutching it, tender yet firm. Then kissed her deeply.

Her body went limp and his body went hard. It held her up.

"Why you here?" he asked, his body holding hers.

Louisa didn't know how to answer the question. In that moment, she wasn't sure why she was in Venice or here with Matteo or why she met with Massimo. She refused to admit to Matteo that she was indeed a candle in the wind, or that his comment stung her. Bad.

To her delight, Massimo appeared at her side and motioned for Matteo to leave.

Matteo didn't move except to bat eyelashes at Louisa over his cigarette.

"I said move," she thought she heard Massimo say but she didn't see him move his mouth. Perhaps it was the strength of his look? His strong presence spoke those words? She wasn't sure.

She thought she heard Matteo reply to Massimo, without moving his mouth either, "She's mine. Get out of here. This is no business of yours."

Louisa often thought she could read Matteo's mind, especially if she was confused or distraught about something. Matteo had insisted he could read her mind and that she could read him as well. She wondered if she were doing so now.

"Stop it," Matteo said to Louisa. "Stop reading us."

"Shut up, fool," Massimo told him. "Don't you have somewhere to go, Matteo, like work," which was not a question but an order said with volume and a tone that screamed *"run along now poor boy."*

Louisa wondered about the details of how Massimo knew Mattro, but she'd been told many times that Venetians knew everyone else in Venice. They loved to learn about their neighbors. Personal dramas were their favorites. She wouldn't have been surprised if Massimo had witnessed personal drama between Matteo and Louisa in the past.

More likely, Matteo's previous run-ins with the law had familiarized them with each other.

Louisa could see that Massimo's command had infuriated Matteo. She'd seen fury in Matteo's eyes many times before, but she'd never seen him keep it at bay nor follow another man's order. Except his father's and then only after much argument, threats or bribery.

Yet he didn't argue with Massimo. Matteo began to walk away and slowed only to say, "Watch yourself Louisa."

"You might want to follow his advice," said Massimo. "That man is danger to you," she also heard Massimo's voice say, but this time Louisa was sure his mouth had not moved. Then slowly, as if gliding, Massimo started to move away but not before he lifted his Prada hat off his head and handed it to her, grinning the most beautiful smile she'd ever seen in all of Italy.

From afar, she then felt Massimo kiss her, strongly and squarely on the mouth.

Neither his lips nor even his body had moved.

QUARTRE (4)

All Play and No Work

That Prada man, the mysterious one. He'd sent Matteo whimpering off with a wrist flick and a stare. He blocked Matteo from her but also stood between her and the information she wanted.

Or thought she wanted? Did she care what happened to the dead glassmakers? Any more than as a passing curiosity? As a tourist hoping to engage in a murder mystery vacation?

No. She didn't care.

Just because the San Marco bells rang when she was thinking about ghosts then rang again when she read the article about the deaths -- which seemed to tell her to look into the deaths and the ghost stories -- didn't mean she cared. And just because Massimo, the Prada man, told her to stay away from the case, and Matteo's brother-in-law worked for the same factory as the two dead men, didn't mean that Louisa had acquired an interest, did it? It didn't mean she wanted to investigate further. Did she?

In the middle of these reflections, Louisa realized she'd been standing at the desk of the secretary to the Venice police chief, staring into a bowl of fancy-wrapped chocolates.

"Let me know if you'd like *one*," the perfect woman behind the desk said in that subtle manner that Louisa had come to believe was her clever way of making all her words belie their meaning. Thus, in offering the chocolate to Louisa, she offered her nothing. First, she'd emphasized the word *one*, only one, as if to say, "Don't you dare take one, but if you dare, it better be only one, if that." Second, why would Louisa need to let her know if she'd like one when the chocolates sat on the desk being offered to anyone? Third, and most important, she'd curled her upper lip when she said it in obvious disapproval of Louisa eating a chocolate and of Louisa, period.

Whichever way Louisa responded, it was a defeat. Louisa wanted that chocolate, the gourmet Swiss milk variety, the gooey caramel centered expensive chocolate you could rarely find. Yet no respectable perfect Venetian woman would herself eat a piece of chocolate in front of another woman. Especially an American woman, a lovely and intelligent professional American woman who outranked her in the police department because of her legal education and outranked her in the Italian male-acquiring department because she'd been born in that superpower country, that most superior of all the superpowers, the almighty America. Therefore, a super powerful American woman could never eat chocolate, ever. Especially not in front of a perfect Venetian woman.

She looked up at the police chief's secretary, whose name Louisa knew but by which she would never call her because the police chief's secretary would be forever referred to by Louisa and her friends as "that perfect woman" or more appropriately "that perfect bitch."

Louisa stood there, hoping to look tough, powerful. Wanting to be seen as an even bigger bitch than the police chief's secretary. To show no emotion, no shame, no insecurity, guilt or even cockiness and to simply be a blank slate. Yet the best she could muster was a squeamish smile, a smirk. Luckily, as always in Venice, an admirer rescued her.

A young man pressed his muscular chest against Louisa's back. He said, "*Si, si, si, signorita, va bene, va bene,*" as he placed one hand on her shoulder then picked up a chocolate with the other hand, deftly peeled off its golden wrapper with the same hand he held it in, let the wrapper drop onto the perfect woman's desk and popped the chocolate into Louisa's eager awaiting mouth.

"Good eh?" he said.

Louisa shook her head in agreement and with eyes closed, she tilted her head into his hand on her shoulder. She didn't chew. She let the chocolate melt between her lips and imagined the perfect woman's face with mouth agape and horrified eyes. Louisa also envisioned pouring the entire bowl of candy onto the perfect head then watch as the gilded packaging toppled over and about her impeccable body like an unwelcome rain shower.

When Louisa opened her eyes, the woman's eyes were not full of horror but glee. While staring into Louisa's eyes she scooped up the wrapper, crumbled and tossed it behind her then turned and smashed it into the marble floor with the knife-like pointed toes of her designer stilletos. To make sure the wrapper was dead, she twisted her heel into it too.

"Is that the best you have?" Louisa said, her renewed power heightened by the handsome rescue. When she said it, she glanced at both the murderous shoes and the crushed, killed wrapper.

"*Scusi?*" said the chocolate wrapper murderess. Louisa had insulted her overpriced shoes. She muttered a Venetian profanity that told Louisa to go wipe her ass on the side of a canal. She rustled papers, slammed desk drawers. Then she vanished with all of the chocolates.

Only her once perfectly heeled, now offensive shoes remained. In the trash.

꩜

"Detective Menetto," said her rescuer. He introduced himself while he kept a brisk pace away from the police chief's office.

"Louisa Mangotti."

"*Bella. Italiana?*"

"*Si,*" she lied. She was not full Italian. Her father's grandfather did immigrate from Italy but her mom was German.

"Mrs. Mangotti," he began.

"I'm not married," Louisa corrected. Detective Menetto had addressed her earlier as *signorita* but perhaps he'd only referred to her by that title to further annoy the keeper of the chocolates, a woman who stood guard outside the door of his domineering boss. Or maybe he'd used that title because he hoped Louisa was single and wished it to be confirmed.

"*Mi scusi*," he said as he bowed. Next he double-air kissed her cheeks, which kisses found more of her cheeks than air. "Can I help you find something?"

The question could refer to many things but, like many English phrases that Italian men uttered, above all else it conveyed a sexual connotation. Louisa thought about the answer for a moment. Oh yes he could help her find something, like the *discoteca,* which she'd learned did not mean the disco at all but more accurately translated to a frolic. Not necessarily a frolic at a disco either but wherever most convenient for one to make merry. Perhaps in a disco, perhaps not, but more likely, in a car. There being no cars in Venice, then a boat. Really just about anywhere could be a *discoteca.*

She knew he could help her find a disco and more but what she couldn't say was that she wanted him to help her find out who might've wanted the glassmakers dead or who may've sent her messages disguised as ghost missives because she didn't know yet if she could trust him. A look of pleasure graced his face at the pause in her answering him and he cocked his head and raised his eyebrows in anticipation of helping her with whatever she needed. She realized he probably thought she was a tourist, possibly there to report a pick-pocketing or lost passport.

"You don't know, do you," she asked in Italian. This intrigued him. An American woman who spoke Italian with a very good accent and who knew something he didn't know. A secret. The equivalent of a Venetian jackpot. "No?" she asked again.

A secret? One which he could be the first to tell everyone, to release it into the foggy Venetian air, to feed and fill the mill. Unlike normal gossip mills, Venetians didn't change the stories they heard as they retold them. Like their home town itself, stories stayed mostly the same throughout the centuries. This secret would be a veritable tape recorded deposition when passing through Venetian circles. That is why secrets were adored by Venetians. Secrets could never be gossip for they were always the truth.

"*Dimmi, dimmi tutto,*" he requested and indeed she planned to tell him everything just as he had asked for but not yet.

He thought about what the secret might be and imagined it moving through the circles: *Louisa Mangotti, Signorita Mangotti, una bella Americana, padre Italiano, madre Italiana*. So on and on, word for word it would go. No detail left out, no amplification of any part, except for those that made the storyteller look better. For example, in Detective Menetto's version of the events that had recently transpired, he would pop not one but many chocolates into her mouth. He would dance around the desk and pop a few more into the mouth of the perfect woman. Then he would wait patiently while the two women fought over him until he was forced to whisk away Louisa and respectfully bid adieu to the scorned one who would slump into her chair in disgust. To Italians, embellishments such as these were considered closer to truth than falsity.

"I'm here in Venice to help with the Interpol database," she said in a tone that sounded as if she'd said she'd been elected the new president of Italy, which was quite a common occurrence in that country. He reacted in a manner as if being elected president was what she'd reported too.

"Translation," he announced. Rather than try to explain that she knew not enough Italian to translate the entire

Interpol database, but simply knew more Italian than anyone in the office knew English, she simply nodded affirmatively. "We must have it. *Gracie Dio,*" he said with hands in prayer position.

"Thank God? Why?" she said.

"Because the problems in the world is coming to Venice. No, those problems are here now, *dottoressa.*"

She didn't ask what problems he referred to or if there was one in particular that concerned him. She did better than that for she nuzzled him and said, "You are from the South, correct?" Of course he was from Southern Italy. Most Italian policemen were southerners and many were politically connected dark-haired beauties named Menetto.

"*Si,*" he said.

"Naples, Calabria or Sicily?"

"*Tutti.*"

"You are from all of them?"

"Si, yes. I move."

She nuzzled further. Saying he was from all of those places was sort of code for saying *my family just about owns this country.*

"My mother's family was from Calabria," she said.

"*Si, si, Americani e mezze Calabrese.*"

"Yes, half of America is from Calabria. No, not half, all. We move," she said.

More laughter ensued until the perfect woman walked by. Her magnificent over-the-knee leather boots tucked into black jeans caused their instant silence. If there was one thing worse than an Italian woman with a beautiful outfit, it was one who wore two beautiful outfits before noon. Not that Louisa hadn't done that before, but she had never done it so well.

"An important lunch date," the woman said. Her dismissive scan of Louisa's suit said, *You're not invited because you don't have the right clothes.*

To Louisa, *important lunch date* meant that while she worked all afternoon for a pittance, this overpaid snotty bureaucrat would sip wonderful wine, feast on fabulous food and laugh about the stupid American slaving back at the office over ancient computers and office machines that either didn't work or were so slow they seemed to be completely stopped. Also it meant that her important lunch date would wear an Armani suit, Hermes tie, highly buffed Ferrigamo shoes, a Versace shirt and would have the deep blue eyes of a Hawaiian sea, the physique and jaw of a Dolce and Gabbana cover model and would kiss both of her hands between courses then licked her fingers after lunch.

"Very important," said Louisa as she pretended to scribble some fake notes on an invisible notepad, allowing the woman to interpret what this odd comment was about. Louisa looked at the young Menetto and faked more note-taking like a school yard guard soliciting witnesses for a later report to superiors. Louisa watched while the woman straightened her back, which thrust her chest forward and her rump up, and took a deep breath as if preparing to spew flames of fire at Louisa's face. She put on her matching hot pink cashmere gloves, hat and scarf, cinched tighter her short leather jacket belt and didn't dare breath hot air or fire for fear it might add a smidgeon to her waistline. Pleased with her silent display, she iced her luscious lips with frosty, hot pink gloss.

Both women knew who'd won this battle. It was the woman who'd win every battle, always, involving anything to do with fashion. Not Louisa. When she turned back, Menetto was gone.

CINQUE (5)

Two Many Men

When Barbara exited the plane at Venice's Marco Polo airport, she noted that the wolves followed. First one handsome man, then two, then two more, then another two, until there was a pack of Italians of which she could approve, never disapprove. All were grouped together, bound as one for maximum effect, this pack. Not that she hadn't noticed them on the plane, but they were now in parade formation.

Unlike most American males Barbara knew, Italian males and, in particular, Venetians, were not averse to being viewed as mere objects, eye candy, works of art. The Italian heritage, genealogy, duty, birthright demanded to be admired like a fine chiseled statue sculpted by Michelangelo. Although a bit offensive, their conceit enticed her, or at least it did today. *It's playful, it's fun, it's light and airy,* thought Barbara. *It is like cotton candy. Yummy.*

It felt like only yesterday Barbara was playing with her cats outside her home in Seattle. *Oh yea, it was only yesterday,* she reflected as she left the trail of men behind her, found a new one at the Alilaguna boat dock and boarded the ferry for Lido, one of many lovely islands off Venice. Barbara picked a hotel on Lido across the lagoon because she wanted an escape, a little breather, from the crowds of St. Mark's Square and Venice proper. She also wanted a buffer zone from Louisa, who didn't know that Barbara arrived a day early and she could rest before the rush began -- the run around with Louisa over bridges, different islands and campos, churches and cemeteries looking for ghosts.

Lido, which means beach in Italian, boasts not only a beach that runs the length of the island, but unlike Venice, it has cars, bicycles, a golf course, roads for motor vehicles and the famous film festival. Like Venetians, people who live on the Lido possess a flawless appearance, maybe more so because they don't have to walk everywhere and they can wear finer threads than the Venetians who must battle the elements.

The men seemed familiar to her, not in a local way but in a New York City boroughs way, N.Y.P.D. brawny cop kind of way, their American cousins. Slicked-back dark hair battled with shaved-bald soccer heads, long-lashed bedroom eyes topped plenty of the universally sculpted noses displayed over full lips and of course, there were the ubiquitous tight pants and hunky, macho walk that said, *I'm too sexy for my pants,* to anyone who looked, which was everyone. These men all silently screamed, *I'm a Latin lover,* in their very body language, their torso led by their crotch. Barbara chuckled remembering what her friend used to say about men in Italy, "They're always touching themselves down there, I think to draw the eyes in that direction."

They all were wearing plenty of jewelry too. Bracelets, chains, rings, earrings, flashy belt buckles with those tight jeans.

To show off their genetically superior round little rumps, concluded Barbara. *Magnifico.*

Soon more man parades would appear for Carnival, a true spectacle not only of costumed revelers but also of interesting spectators, scores of gorgeous men from all over the world. It was like being backstage with male models during fashion week. Days before Carnival, Barbara noticed that where there was one, there were many as the men continued to travel in packs of at least two, usually three or more.

Barbara wondered what she would do first. *Go to the next boat dock, get to the hotel room, paint the toes, then paint the town?* she thought. *Need to go into Venice. Immediamente.*

Barely arrived on Lido and Venice called her. She was ready to answer, to go where the world wasn't in transit. Strange how quickly Barbara tired of cars, trees, bicycles. She longed to go back in time, where nothing changed. *Ah Venezia. Mi amore.* Although happy to be near the beach, she nonetheless missed the bustle of San Marco, Dorsodoro, Santa Croce and the other of the six sestiere (sections) of Venice proper with a wider range of distractions than here on quiet Lido.

Okay then, refresh my Italian, pronto. Avvocato. Lawyer. Sorella, sister. Provare, to try. Trovare, to find. Barbara, who always confused those two words, practiced mentally. *Should not 'provare' be 'to prove'? I guess 'to try' will prove whether its right or wrong. And trova? How to remember that one? Treasure trove?*

She spied some locals who could've been her cousins, uncles, sisters, aunts. A tale of two cultures. She deliberated on how Italians remember loyalties, to their friends, to their family, to their cousins in America. She thought of how Paris was so different. *Do the French remember? Do they not want to admit many of them have moved to America too? Or do they stifle it, stiffen and rebel?* Barbara mulled it all over while riding the *vaporetto* to the other end of Lido, which was not really Lido at all but rather Mallamoco, a separate island connected by a bridge. *Italians embrace, dance, sing, celebrate. French watch, listen. Strange, the difference in the two cultures, sharing a border, a Latin heritage, a romantic desire, but articulated in very distinct ways.*

She identified a French couple in the boat by their guidebook and secretly praised them for maintaining their stubborn, authoritative difference while at the same time shaming them for frankly forgetting their francophile ways when they tried to be like the Italians whom, Barbara had observed, the French often venerated. *Viva Italia! Which Latin culture seems more like us?* Barbara wondered, although the answer was obvious to her for she had pigeonholed the French.

At the *vaporetto* stop, she saw a toddler in a stroller dressed in a cat costume and remembered her first Venice Carnival. Louisa had told her tales of it before she experienced it herself--of the extravagantly costumed marauders dressed such that one could not tell if they were man or woman. To be sure the already exquisite Italians needed no such enhancements. Bedecked in their satisfied selves and of course, black leather, they stood out as a parade to be as much reckoned with as did the masked merrymakers at Carnival.

Bacio. Give me a kiss. Kiss, kiss, cheek, cheek, hug, hug, European style, she recalled spending youthful time here. At the restaurants, whether it was lunch or dinner, are you kidding, it was dreamland. She never knew why she had to travel twelve hours by plane to experience such a feeling of radiance. *Magnifico.*

The sun warmed her and thawed her nose during the breezy boat ride. *It is usually sunny in Italy too.* Maybe the Italian sunshine explained the distraction, her need to be here. Maybe not. How could anything fully clarify her pure selfish joy to be a traveler, a wanderer, the watcher, the watched?

On the way to her hotel, she stopped to sit on small bench in the unreal setting. With the lagoon shore behind it, purple wisteria hung along a brick wall like delicate golden ringlets, locks donned with purple flowered bows. Barbara closed her eyes and listened. She heard someone singing a tune in a strong Italian accent: "All da lonely people where do dey all come from? All da lonely people, where do dey all belong, Ah look at all da lonely people."

Did any of "da lonely people" came from Italy, Barbara wondered. It was hard for her to imagine that possibility. *The Italians, they're a happy people,"* she remembered one of her Italian relatives told her. *The German half of me, from an unhappy people?*

She wondered if this odd combination made her crazy. Her German blood, the "do what you are told and do it efficiently" variety, mixed with Italian blood. The "do what you are told but only if you want to do it and maybe do it tomor-row and only if you do not find a reason to disagree with it" kind of blood.

I require strict guidance. With room to rebel. Happy, not lonely, in her family of hundreds of relatives. Coddled, con-fused, insisted, teased and tormented but never left alone.

"Died in da church, buried her long wit da name, nobody come," the singer continued.

Be thankful for your relentlessly loving sister. Someone will come to the church, she reflected. *I may be alone this minute, but someone will come along, my new best friend. Should be arriving any time now.*

"Venice is dirty," Barbara overheard an American tourist say to her companion as both looked around at the marvelous lagoon. Despite the overwhelming beauty that surrounded them here in Venice, some tourists noticed only the strewn trash on a windy day. Barbara knew they would return home and tell everyone that Venice is dirty. *I heard it is dirty, isn't Venice dirty?* Everyone would repeat it, over and over, when they'd never even been to Venice.

It didn't matter. Dirty or clean, smelly or not, people came from all over the globe for as long as this strange lagoon town has existed. If they cannot go to Venice, they fondly dream of it.

Barbara wanted to yell out to the two Americans: *Every day they pick up your garbage, from you tourists, who arrived to see wind blown trash, your trash, strewn about,* for Barbara was already thinking of herself as a local, not a tourist.

After she checked into her hotel and into a sexy shirt, tight jeans and high heels, she clicked along the cobblestones to find an Italian restaurant like the ones in the movies. With red checkered tablecloths, baskets of bread and carafes of wine.

Soon she spotted one of those restaurants and inside she also spotted a dark-haired, blue-eyed, fine jawed man across the room. Her eyes must have lingered on him for a split second longer than usual because when she looked again he stared intensely back into her eyes. Although she pretended indifference, he knew better. *I saw you see me*, his eyes said to Barbara, who loved this about Venetian men--admire them and they admire back without fail. It is all they want or ask in return. To be admired. It made them happy and her smile.

Her smile made him lean forward to insure eye contact was complete and effective. With eye contact confirmed, she continued with her meal as she conversed with an English-speaking couple at the adjoining table. People often asked how it was that she would be eating alone? Why did she travel alone and was she afraid of being *pinched* by the men? She laughed and told the young couple, "my friends back home say I should have a golden trash can for the phone numbers of eligible foreign men that I throw away."

As if by design, the waiter interrupted at that moment and said, "*Signorita,* two men there would like you have a drink with them?"

"Well," she said to the couple, "looks like I've got some phone numbers to collect."

The couple half-laughed in total amazement while Barbara asked for an espresso and waved thanks to both the men. By now her admirer's companion had also turned to see her. The men responded to her wave with "tsk, tsk," followed by a scolding index finger and an insistent motion for her to join them.

So she did. *If you insist.*

Giavanni (or Gianni, the architect) and Sebastiano, (or Seba, cafe owner) leaned towards her from opposite sides of the table. With her in the middle, each grinned and patted the top of her hand nearest to them. Her heart skipped. She turned to each man, then back again to the English-speaking couple with a look of bafflement at the timing as well as at the difficulty in choosing between the two men.

While not as handsome as Gianni, cafe owner Seba sported wonderful piercings, a soccer body, a stylish crinkled white shirt, fitted vest, jeans that surely cost hundreds and a snake-skin belt hooked with a skeleton buckle prominently placed to draw attention to where he obviously knew all eyes should rightly be. She could see that money was no object when it came to clothes for this Italian.

Her attraction first gravitated to Seba, the shyer, less aggressive of the two, who appealed to her in a silent sweet way. But Gianni was tall, dark and like a photo-shopped, airbrushed movie-star. So she decided . . . to be undecided.

The evening progressed and like an observer at a tennis match, she continued to move her head back and forth to each man. She sat between them while they doted on her. No gorgeous Italian women could disturb their attention to Barbara. No hip-high boots, false eyelashes or tight skirts could match this intriguing, raven-haired American. Bar after bar they hopped, which produced the same result--their fixed concentration on Barbara regardless of the quality of the competition.

For some reason it surprised her when they asked her to be the judge of a kissing match. In hindsight, it seemed a likely move on their part. Seba kissed her first with soft demure. Gianni made her whimper with his passion. She declared Seba the narrow winner, which served only to incite Gianni to insist upon a rematch. No arm-twisting needed there, Barbara obliged it. This time, Seba landed a close second when Gianni's passionate kiss ended in soft touches on her lips. This prompted a 'two out of three' with no end in sight.

Sometime during the evening, they made known that both men were available to her, in any way she required, and both at the same time, if preferred. Few American males she knew would consent to such a thing. If the threesome involved two women, they might be interested. The three-way offer reminded Barbara of the whole "Italian men want to be like women" thing. When Barbara said, "Italian men secretly want to be women," Gianni replied, "no not secretly."

Two men? Two quality ones at that? Offering themselves together for one woman, Barbara? How could this be? How could this be happening?

How can this be happening to me? How splendid, she thought with mental delight.

She asked Gianni why they would consent to having her together and he struggled for an English word to answer. He asked for her Italian-English dictionary then pointed to the word *eccitante*. It meant "exciting."

Seba didn't speak a word of English and looked perplexed by her discourse with Gianni about this extraordinary offer *to be three*, as he called it. Seba watched and waited while Gianni refused to translate and courted her in broken English. Seba spoke to her without words.

Barbara realized a battle for her solo attention was on, just in case she didn't go for the three-way. As if by magic, they transported her to Gianni's nearby apartment. At the threshold, she could see that the tiny two room flat held an imposing bed that filled one room with small shower conveniently next to it. On the threshold began an innocent, sort of passionate, sort of thing. Nuzzling and kissing, not really fooling around, the men tried to persuade her to come inside. She tried to stop it.

Outside Gianni's apartment, Barbara snuggled the two distinct but equally charming men. Clothes would not be removed. She would not go in his house. Yet, the night so far, and the thought of taking it further, awakened her inside as these two romantic strangers wooed her, pulled her in two directions.

She chose to claim her sexuality for herself. Her hot, newfound sexy, confident, self.

So Barbara eventually refused their tempting invitation to get naked with both of them.

Her decision to leave caused much heated persuasion from Gianni and sad puppy-dog glances from Seba. Flattered but cautious, she had to leave or else a Venetian orgy goddess might somehow be invoked, sweeping her into moments of lovemaking with two handsome and willing men. She might then forget any morals she once professed and go for it.

She headed for the *vaporetto* but Seba followed, leaving Gianni with the sad glances this time. She departed with the non-English speaking Seba, not a necessary word between them because the chemistry did the talking as he walked her to the boat. As her boat pushed off from the dock, Seba waved good-bye.

Poor Gianni, she thought. *Yet, there's always tomorrow.*

For I will not throw the phone numbers of Gianni or Seba into the golden trash can.

SEI (6)

Venetian Trudge

Upon awakening, Barbara heard the clatter of raindrops clang onto clay roof shingles. *Shoot. Today I've got to move myself and drag two suitcases across the beach island, climb over several bridges and clippety-clop the cobblestones to the boat dock then ferry across the lagoon then up the Grand Canal and wrestle the suitcases out of the ferry through the maze over more bridges and cobblestones to Louisa's apartment.*

She could go back to sleep, wake before breakfast ended and if it was still raining after a breakfast of Nutella, yogurt, red orange juice and many cappuccinos, she could turn on the British news, open the shutters to fill the room with fresh damp air, repack the mess she made in one night on Lido and decide whether to go out.

As the coffees kicked in or the rain subsided, the sun might shine and she could strip down to a tank top for the arduous haul to Louisa's flat in the city.

๛◎๛

Like most mornings in Venice this February, Louisa woke to the sound of rushing water. Was it raining heavily? Was her apartment flooded? Were the gutters pouring out their overload? Were the rubbish collectors hosing down the pavement? Louisa never knew for sure what the rushing water was that she often heard outside her door until she peered outside. Even then what she saw was questionable given the usually foggy, shadowy Venetian light. Her morning stroll could mean trudging through flooded streets in pouring rain. Often meant carrying heavy packages over bridge upon bridge. Frequently it resulted in meeting someone for whom she wanted to be dressed impeccably, even in the rain. Looking good in an impossible situation was the norm.

Louisa had to get out of her apartment, not for coffee, but to visit one of Matteo's sisters. If she went to the hotel where Ana worked, Louisa might extract a bit of information from her without running into Matteo. She remembered Massimo's warning her about Matteo, *that man is danger to you,* every time she placed that warm, fine Prada hat on her head, which was all day, every day. Louisa struggled to shake off the memory of two men whose verbal tussling she had not imagined but had witnessed--that of her usually unflappable ex-boyfriend against a wealthy stranger. The rushing water outside her door soon became louder and she moved to the door to listen. This morning it turned out to be the garbage collectors cleaning the pavement and fortunately, no flooding.

Every day is garbage day in this remarkable town. Every evening Venetians carefully place recycled grocery bags full of trash outside, on the handles of their doors to avoid tampering by rats, cats or floods. Louisa smiled when she recalled the notice the owner of her rented apartment had posted on her kitchen wall:

> *GARBAGE--Due to the quite unusual disposition of Venice, disposing of garbage is more difficult than in normal city centers. So please put your garbage bags on the bridge facing the Palazzo (palace) 6 to 8 am; it will be cleaned up in the morning between 6 and 8. JUST FASTENED BAGS!!! Thank you*

Today, as always, the corps of collectors spread out across the city to accomplish the "unusual disposition" of garbage. They removed plastic bags from door handles or bridges, built mounds of trash in barges waiting in the nearest canals and hosed cigarette butts and other debris off the pavement. Louisa could spend the better part of a morning observing the impressive details of this operation.

This *quite unusual disposition of garbage* was even more unusual this morning. The lively laughs and vulgar Venetian jokes of the street cleaners were suddenly interrupted by the squeal of an unsuspecting passerby. The poor fellow had turned a corner directly into the street-cleaners' hoses and his consequential response to getting soaked was equally Venetian, thus vulgar, as well. *"Cazzo de merda,"* swore the accidental victim. Louisa chuckled at hearing this early comedy and imagined one handsome Venetian dressed in work overalls pointing a hose at a fashionably dressed and equally handsome drenched man, while she slipped on her rain boots, just in case. She knew that such was the possible fate she faced on her early morning walks.

Trying to dress impeccably for a rainy day wasn't easy but was essential because, as the Venetians say, "When you go out in Venice, it's like visiting someone's living room. Would you dress sloppy to visit someone's home?" It was well-past ten by the time Louisa headed out. Once outside, she stepped lightly as she negotiated the slippery bridges on her way past the school she wasn't attending today, although she was supposed to go into work. She didn't want to get out of bed this morning because the moment she opened her eyes, she concerned herself with something more powerful than the Venetian rushing waters. Matteo.

That man is danger to you, she could hear Massimo say. *Good luck with him for he does have information,* she thought she heard him add before he left.

Be kind to your lovely sister, she then thought she heard Massimo say on her way to the Danieli hotel today. That was impossible. Massimo wasn't with her and he hadn't met her sister who was back home in Seattle. Louisa stopped abruptly, looked around and saw nobody. She knew Venetians were clever at hiding, watching.

"Matteo spying on me. He thinks he can intimidate, stop me from doing what I want with my life," she said out loud while walking past several Venetians who smiled with glee at the drama she created for them. Maybe she would chug a double cappuccino in front of them too and consciously violate their unwritten Italian rule of "no cappuccino after breakfast." Violating any rule, especially an Italian one, was in order this morning. Perhaps a drink was in order too.

Walking into the coffee shop immediately relaxed her, not because of the relaxing environment there, but because her mood lifted whenever she entered a Venetian cafe. She ordered a double espresso with a shot of Zambuca on the side. The bartender didn't balk. He noticed her flushed cheeks and figured they were from cold, rain or agitation and hurried to accommodate her. The pit of her stomach fluttered when she thought about coffee houses in America that never felt the same as a Venetian or even Parisian one. Any cafe anywhere in France or Italy for that matter. They gave her a sense of ease and comfort and the Zambuca would add to it.

There at the bar, with her warm liquor and cappuccino, she began to daydream. She saw herself sitting outside in the sun at the Florian Cafe, classical music serenaded her, a handsome man asked her all about herself. He wore his beautiful Italian outfit and in his sexy Italian accent he asked for her phone number.

Her phone rang. In the midst of the fabulous daydream. It was Matteo. She suspected that his sister Ana hadn't wasted any time getting the Venetian telegram out to him to let him know Louisa was planning a stop at the hotel where she worked.

"*Pronto?*" she said as if she didn't know who was calling

"You're back in Venice," he said and after a long pause he added "Again. Why?" Never one to avoid conflict or judgments, he made his points quick and blunt. It was Matteo's best weapon. Mean and tactless, blunt discourse.

Prepared by years of therapy, law school and Barbara's training, she remained stoic. "Yes" was all she said, but she thought, *You have the right to remain silent, Louisa. Anything you say, can and will, no, forget can, it just will be used against you by Matteo.*

"No work? You never work. Have fun." Guilt, his next weapon.

"Oh I will," she said and nothing more. *Don't admit, admit, admit. Don't explain, explain, explain,* she told herself like she'd been taught to tell clients if accused of a crime.

"Your sister? Barbara? Why she come here? Will be bad for her here." Someone had spilled the beans about Barbara's trip and those proverbial beans now lay scattered across the porcelain tile in front of Louisa in the quaint Venetian bar. He'd used the fear weapon. A powerful one. It often left Louisa defenseless. Match, game, set. He set up the chess pieces, slowed for the ambush. Once he had her sniveling, trembling, anxious and grieved, he'd surround her. He would move back in for the kill. Checkmate.

No, not checkmate yet. Louisa paused then waived at the bartender for another drink. He rushed to get it, eavesdropping as they did in Venice and reading her reactions, he knew that an Italian man had called her in Venice and she was not pleased about it. Matteo was using the fear weapon and that one, the fear weapon, was a good one. Matteo would do a full court press with it if given the chance. But Louisa knew that Matteo feared something too and, although she wasn't sure what it was, she was sure that the volatile Matteo could be pushed into surrender by pushing the right buttons.

"Barbara will be fine," she said. *A little too much? Trying too hard to sound like everything was okay between Louisa and her sister being here in Venice.* Some people would say that living in Italy while working as a lawyer was an exciting opportunity but to this Venetian, Matteo, firmly rooted into the fertile family soil, it signified pure reckless abandon.

"Oh that is a stupid ting I hear. *Idiota.* Fool with law, drinking half the wine in the Veneto." Louisa was indeed doing just that, this much she couldn't deny. So she didn't. She raised her new shot of Zambuca to the bartender in defiance of Matteo's accusation then gulped it down.

"It's my life," she couldn't believe she said. Stranger still, she meant it. It worked. What followed was a long pause and much sighing from Matteo. "Anything else?" she asked to break the silence and not give him a moment to think of his next move. But the open-ended question could've invited more criticism. Yet, it felt right, something moved her to be bold, assertive. She waited for his response, *Give me everything you've got, right here, right now, because I ain't budging off my position. It's my life. Leave me alone,* she thought. It was a huge bluff.

He bought it. "I will have more to say, *dopo* (later). I go now," he said. But he hadn't hung up on her. He waited for her next move.

Liar, she thought. *I won round one. That's why you 'go now.'* Then, from the depths of her newly accessed self-assured self, and aided by a third shot of Zambuca, Louisa added, "Can you believe how lucky we are?"

She'd been taught to know the perfect final question for a cross-examination -- a question that didn't require an answer to win, to pin the witness. It doesn't require a response because no matter what the witness answers, the jury looks pitifully at them, knowing they're sunk. With raised eyebrows, the questioner can simply give the jury the "I got 'em" look. Any answer -- yes, no, maybe -- it is all the same. The jury, unified with the questioner against the witness, waits. The lawyer always says, "No further questions. You may step down."

What was Matteo's response? Yes, no, maybe?

"*Cazzo,*" he swore at her and hung-up.

"No further questions. You may step down," Louisa said to her imaginary jury, knowing she'd won an important round with a hostile witness. Matteo.

The bartender heard her and nodded in agreement. Italians must stick together in the fight against oppression from family or foe. "We love it, *si o no?*" she said to the bartender to confirm his allegiance.

"*Si,*" said the bartender as he slammed down two shots, one for him and one for her.

෨◎෭

Louisa had a slight problem. Barbara planned to stay with her while in Venice but perhaps Matteo would be hanging around. Louisa hoped to avoid his advances recalling Massimo's warning again, yet her resolve began to wear off when the Zambuca did not.

As her mind began to wander, she observed her friendly Italian bartender. She needed a bigger apartment to hold the egos of Barbara, Matteo and any new admirer she might want to invite over for, say, coffee or tea.

Her imagination conjured up a likely scenario: Sexy Matteo wormed his way into her heart once he became charming again and he always did. Their fights would fuel lustful flames as they had always done in the past. Thus, the need for privacy. She would feel lonely in Venice at some point. She might need comforting. From a man. Matteo, the easy accessible choice, was also a familiar one. Barbara hated him.

Still she felt those eerie feelings about yesterday's encounter between Matteo and Massimo. Caution had stirred in her. The look of rage in Matteo's face, when he capitulated to a richer man in front of her, was extremely disarming. His surrender to Massimo in her presence perplexed. Barbara's visit could serve as a buffer, would perhaps keep Matteo away and Louisa safer?

After that phone call and with too much Zambuca in her body, she decided to postpone the trip to visit Matteo's sister Ana, walk off the Zambuca and maybe take a nap.

In her walk home, full of strong licorice liquor and preoccupied with Mattteo, Louisa tripped on steps at two bridges and almost toppled into canals.

Not again, no more falling in canals, she thought.

She tried to concentrate on steps, but the alternating wrath and charms of Matteo, which she knew would be forthcoming, continued to preoccupy her. Louisa fell in before, in a canal and in love with Matteo. She feared it would happen again.

She peaked around each dark corner and surveyed the area around her doorstep. She hoped he wasn't there waiting and then she wished he was there waiting. As usual, conflicted about Matteo, she knew her victory with him would be short-lived.

❧

SETTE (7)

Rain

In the quiet *Dorsodoro sestiere*, Louisa looked through the little round windows of her tiny apartment into *Campo San Toma*. The *campo* was empty and no laundry hung on clothes lines. No lingering tourists listened to the quartet that often played in the *campo* next to the cistern. By the time she woke from her short post-Zambucca snooze, the quartet was reduced to a trio because one musician had already packed up to leave.

Cello and violin cases sat open in front of the threesome waiting for an audience to toss coins into them. A single large instrument stood upright next to the now silent fourth musician and caused her to blink. It looked like either a fifth musician or their ghostly manager. Behind them, the doors of one of many churches-turned-museums were bolted shut.

A picture of a clown was posted on a cafe window to advertise mobile phones, but it appeared to Louisa as another ghost, its reflection smiling grimly at the few souls who walked past it.

Devoid of life, the *campo*'s eery scene was typical of a bad-weather day in Venice. In this fog, everything appeared somewhat less than real to Louisa. Soon the music stopped, another musician packed his violin into the awaiting felt-lined case. The mist became another obstacle to making a small salary for their priceless music.

The prediction was for rain.

Rain. A Venetian dilemma. Courtyard cisterns catch rain to provide for Venetian needs. Rain cleans concrete and sweeps pigeon droppings off the pavement. On the other hand, if Venetians must go out when it rains, they must walk through the storms since there are no cars or taxi cabs in which to ride it out. As a result, Venetians know the minute rain will come and they often stay home. Rain produces the water necessary to sustain the lagoon, but it also presents many obstacles, not to mention floods.

Rain, an unwelcome necessity, felt like the favor she would soon need from Matteo. Her encounters with Matteo on this trip had been typical Louisa-Matteo dramas, the kind where, unquestionably drawn to one another, they fed off both love and hate.

She recalled her seeming accidental meeting with him on the ferry. She could never be sure if he had been tipped off by God knows whom to where she was or what she was doing.

That meeting fit perfectly with their tragicomical romantic ways. "Wow. You look so beautiful," he'd whispered in her ear, his Venetian accent sending shivers down her neck. After he focused his attention on getting her excited right there in the boat, he enticed her further with his simple half grin, a lowering of his eye lids and a sideways glance. The whisper felt warm and his breath travelled down her neck, rested on her throat -- she couldn't swallow or speak. Without moving his lips from her ear, in the same soft whisper, he added "those jeans fit you wonderfully." He murmured those words and his breath fell again onto her throat, this time practically choking her. His breath on her neck had said, *I want to grab you right here, kiss you, and you will let me and you will not want to stop.*

Then the drama. The hate. He put her back into conflict when he pulled away a bit and her head unwittingly went with him, glued to his every word, breath and move. His eyes dropped to her formfitting pants and he said sweetly, but with words far from sweet and in his own quintessentially villainous way, "How do you stay fit, after all of these years? How old are you now? Thirty, forty?"

Pow. The knockdown. Was that a loud drum that cracked in her ear? Whatever the age, Matteo rounded it to the higher number, the decade number, the one people celebrated, she knew not why, but the number at which women cringed, the rounded numbers of thirty, forty or fifty and beyond. She didn't correct him to say she was twenty-something -- that would've fed into his game. To argue would've showed him it bothered her. Either way, he won. Forced to lose that round of their unceasing sparring, she'd had no choice but to let it sit. At thirty. Thirty or forty.

She hated him right then just thinking about it.

To shake off thoughts of Matteo, she focused on her view of the *campo* out her window. Two Venetians motioned frantically at each other. They looked up, first at the sky directly above them then all around. Not a cloud, but some-how it told Venetians that it would rain. She could tell they were talking about the forthcoming rain because she saw them motion some more at the sky. Louisa concluded that plans were being made to finish something before the inevitable storm.

For a moment she considered canceling her appointment with Matteo's sister, Ana, on the opposite side of Venice in San Marco. There was no direct route to San Marco from *San Toma* and it was damp and getting colder.

"Venetians are afraid of rain," Louisa once told Barbara.

Understandably so, with floods a looming concern and not all places accessible by boat, every journey involves walking in Venice even during storms. Thus, locals avoid going out when it rains. In a manner typical of Venetian ingenuity, when it rains, everything they need to get done is politely postponed or pawned off on someone who can't say *no*.

Excuses and lies are expected and told:

> *Well, I can't bring those carpet pieces over today, the supplier is late, you know, because of the rain.* To which the reply might be, *I see, of course, tomorrow then, if it's clear.* Cunning and guilt might be employed, *I wish it would stop raining, I'm running out of things, I'll be forced out with this arthritis that flares up in damp weather.* A Venetian might offer help but only because it's inevitable that someday they'll need the favor returned. *I must go out today, you went out last week for me, what can I bring you?* Venetians keep track.

They are like birds perched on a garden gate or tilted chair, a bit off balance but hanging on for so long as necessary. Safely sheltered indoors or under awnings, locals hunkered down until the rain stops.

Many Venetians don't even own rain boots. Most carry plastic bags with which to wrap over their fine Italian shoes. If the forecast calls for rain, it would be very inconvenient, cumbersome even, to carry boots around the mazes and up and down bridges.

Louisa looked back. Her round window surrounded in wood and its glass divided in odd-shaped panes, it gave her a segmented view. She saw the steep roof covered in snow-like lace that hung on the edges of terra cotta arched roof shingles. Like the strands of her hair blown by the heat of her radiator and floated towards the window, the snow whipped in fragmented pieces in the wind and rested on a ledge besides the doors. The house nearest to hers, its roof speckled with white and displaying its dark moldy brick, contrasted with the sun's haphazard rays. Fog drifted over, as it often did here, and created what appeared to be a dusty film on the ground. It blurred and covered dirty snow on her little windows.

Louisa recalled a time when she and Barbara were dining outside with Venetian friends and clouds darkened the skies. Louisa and Barbara eagerly sought shelter but the Venetians refused to move, said, "*aspetta*" (wait) and continued to sip coffee or wine despite threatening skies. Although Louisa and Barbara sat back down, they continued to question whether they should go inside.

The locals, unfazed by the dark sky, remained seated on the terrace and enjoyed their meals and drinks. They motioned for the sisters to stay outside with them. They waved off the rain clouds with calm hand flicks and shoulder shrugs. Then, at once and together, every Venetians on the terrace started to move fast. They rapidly pushed chairs and tables under the awnings. They removed plates, tossed bread into the lagoon, retrieved handbags and satchels in minutes. When the last item was securely covered, everyone stepped inside the cafe. The minute they did so, it poured.

Louisa also knew clotheslines were effective weather vanes. If clothes are hanging, it won't rain, no matter what the cloud coverage seems to say. Venetian mammas know best, better than any weather man. When a Venetian mother empties her clothes line, get out your wading boots, even on a sunny day. Or stay home, like the Venetians. Expect a downpour.

Venetian at heart but a tourist in action, Louisa always went out despite the rain. In the worst of storms, motivated tourists wanted to see Venice, to view it in the rain, to experience high water, to watch people wade around in boots. Whenever San Marco Square floods, tourists do not stay stuck in their rooms, especially when on a mission and all tourists are on impossible missions to see all of Venice in a day. Even in the rain.

Today Louisa was on a mission of a different sort. Soaked to the knees after trudging across Venice, she entered the Danieli. Originally part of the Doge's royal palace, the Danieli luxury hotel faces the lagoon with a striking view of San Giorgio Island and its bell tower. Danieli history is prestigious yet sordid, involving stories about Richard Wagner, Henry James, Casanova and other luminaries associated with her glorious past and present fame.

Dutifully posed at the front desk, Matteo's young sister, Ana, greeted Louisa the instant she walked through the revolving doors. Beaming, she said, "*Ciao cara bella. Sono contento tu sei quoi,*" (Hello dear beauty, I am happy you are here.)

"*Ciao mori, come stai,* (Hello friend, how are you) said Louisa.

"*Bene, bene, et tu, come stai?*" (Very well, and you?)

"*Bene, gracie.*

The formalities were ended with hugs, air kisses and giggles then Louisa decided to ask about a room for Barbara and forget this whole business of ghosts, Matteo and murder.

"Okay, I wait for your sister," said Ana. Without any prompting, she quickly added, "Is amazing. I want to know everything about your ghost. I'm interested. Hi hi hi hi." Then with raised brows, she blinked her eyes and flapped her hands around like butterflies.

Louisa had not told Ana, nor Matteo for that matter, about the ghosts, so who did? Nothing seemed a secret in this town. "If I reserve a room for my sister, can she have a canal view," said Louisa, ignoring Ana's reference to ghosts. "Let me see, which date?"

"For the room is okay, okay by canal. And you know my sister sees ghosts, like your sister," she said with a matter of fact tone as if she and Louisa had been discussing ghosts for hours. Not prying nor knowingly superior like Matteo would say do it, she offered, "Maybe a discount for the room? I don't know, I have to ask for the manager, she control price plan. Mmm ... ghosts? Mmm ... anyway, for the room, soon as possible if you want it you can book just sending an email."

Louisa was now annoyed with the entire conversation. Ana asked questions that Louisa was supposed to be asking.

Ana began to interrogate and offer information instead of Louisa doing it while slyly pretending to be there to reserve a room for Barbara. "I can reserve the room on the website and get the discount then maybe you can give her the canal view if I ask for it. Yes?"

"Yes. Your sister's trip, is about the ghosts in Venice?"

Louisa found it harder and harder to refrain from asking Ana how she knew about the ghosts so she paused for a second to look directly into her eyes. She saw the answer. Ana learned it from Matteo, who knew everything. He most likely knew exactly when Louisa had arrived in Venice, where she was living, who she was associating with and what she was doing there. Ana's knowing but concerned look said, *be careful with Matteo,* although Louisa recalled that Ana in the past had naively thought that all would be fine between the two lovers.

Ana peeked over Louisa's shoulder through the windows of the revolving door and became very busy with papers. She gave Louisa not a nervous glance but rather a compliant stance, one obedient not to the job but to whatever or whomever she saw outside. *Matteo?*

Louisa clung to the hope of not being used again by Matteo or at least to the hope of resisting him. She ignored his sway on Ana and was emboldened. She decided to get the information she came for, despite whatever had been already said by Ana or anything that might have transpired outside the hotel's revolving door.

"Yes, I am doing research about the ghosts of Venice," said Louisa, "and I want Angelica to tell me some stories about the hauntings in Murano," said Louisa.

Matteo's older sister, Angelica, had been very close to Matteo until she married into a prestigious glassmaking family. Angelica, whose manner contradicted her name, led a life a crime with her brother during their teen years. The striking Angelica was also extremely jealous of Matteo as the only male offspring and primary heir to her father's fortune in vineyards and other real estate holdings. When she married into the glassmaking family, it took her up a few notches in status and pitted her husband, Marco Demario, against her brother, Matteo. Thus, began one of those Venetian dramas that stemmed from wealth and influence, of which everyone never seemed to have enough. Angelica might be married to a rich and powerful man, but she also wanted the inheritance her father would bequeath to Matteo, unless he totally fucked it up.

"Isn't there a ghost, a *fantasme*, in your sister's new house in Murano?" Louisa asked. "I remember a ghost that Angelica used to see."

"Ahm ... yea ... they says there was too much ghosts in Murano houses. And hers cause the home was a ... eham ... a nazist tower. I don't know how to explique," offered Ana using the best English she knew.

A sharply dressed waiter walked by carrying a silver tray topped with crystal flutes and a plate of cheeses. Louisa had an idea. She put her finger up to Ana, a gesture for her to wait a second while she reserved a table for lunch near the piano. Louisa, certain that Matteo awaited her exit outside, intended to foil any plot to ambush her. Or whatever was the plan. Something was going on here that she had to fight. The game was on.

"I want to know all about the Murano ghosts, the nazi tower, everything. Where can I find this history of her

Murano house? And a history of nazis in Murano? What is the name of the Murano house? I can go research."

"There's nothing, I think, public. About the house. Maybe in the *municipio*?"

"The municipal office on Murano Island? What about your family?

"My family I think maybe knows something or Angelica's husband," Ana said, who seemed not the least bit concerned with this conversation or about telling Louisa anything she knew of the Murano ghosts. Ana didn't want to give too much information but she would offer enough to clue her in, to help Louisa figure it out, thereby protecting herself yet informing Louisa. Ana kept providing details and her enthusiasm increased with each new question.

Louisa wondered about Ana's motives.

"What house was a nazi tower?" asked Louisa. "When? What is the name of the calle, the street?"

Ana eyes moved sideways, glanced towards the front door then she said, "I don't know that."

Oh, but you do know that, and much more, thought Louisa.

"Okay, this is good information," said Louisa. "I miss your family. Say hello to Angie, to everyone, from me," she said.

She planned to walk away since Ana had clammed up but Ana, as if talking about hotel room reservations or giving directions to a customer, laid a map of Murano on the counter in front of Louisa. She pointed to a spot on the map near to the lighthouse, known as *Faro*. What she then said didn't reference either the map or the beacon.

"When I was young I saw one ghost in the house. I heard one girl singing." Ana took a deep breath and appeared removed from the hotel. She seemed to be listening to the song of this ghostly girl. "I was really scare," said Ana using the wrong tense of the word.

"What did the ghost look like?" asked Louisa. She had not known that Matteo's family had lived in Murano in the past. Matteo's connection to the dead glassmakers just got stronger.

"Mmm ... white. She was praying, but she was without face. The face was completely black."

"Is that why you were scared? Because her face was black?"

"You know, she were like Maria when were born Jesus. Yes, cause when I saw her I get out from the bed and she look at me." In her mind, Ana was clearly in that place where the vision took place, her home in Murano, not standing before Louisa at the Danieli Hotel. "I run to my mother," she finished.

Louisa could see Ana consciously lose the haunted vision and return consciously to the front desk where rows of slots for keys sat behind her, room numbers under each one. She lifted a key and handed it to the guest who had walked up and requested it for that room number.

"*Mia mamma*," Ana began in Italian then decided to switch to English, "is always speaking of you." She gently rubbed both of Louisa's hands. "My mother holds everyday the small book you gave her." Ana, a darling teenager who graduated high school the previous spring, spoke English well but with an occasional wrong tense or missing word.

"What is the small book that I gave her?"

"Mmm something about a, mmm, *angelo custode?* It's small, small, small."

"Oh, I think I remember now," said Louisa. She recalled the book she'd given to Matteo's mother years ago, a little book in Italian about angels. His mother said Louisa was an angel sent from God to save her son from his addictions and criminal inclinations. His mother had been wrong.

Ana checked her watch. "Darling, I go eat," she said, but not to stall or avoid the conversation. To the contrary, she wanted very much to continue telling Louisa about the Murano ghosts, but it was lunch time.

Italians never work past this countrywide, almost legally imposed, unspoken yet understood, lunch deadline.

"Okay, I go eat too," Louisa said and pointed to the restaurant. She started to follow the host to her agreed upon table. "We talk later," Louisa said in unintended, unconscious, broken English.

Ana was already out the door, not wanting to miss the imposing lunch deadline.

Yes, the lunch deadline.

The mere thought of ghosts, haunted hotel rooms, Matteo and murder made Louisa hungrier and she wanted to eat more of the fabulous food they would spread before her. Very expensive food, she would relish at the Danieli, in its welcoming drawing room.

The lobby boasted a stairwell of marble, intricately detailed with all manor of flourishes as was everything at this hotel. Bright and cheery, even on a foggy day, the lobby restaurant possessed a huge ceiling that beamed plenty of illumination through its ornate, hand-blown, stained-glass skylight.

At night, however, the Danieli sometimes played the part of a haunted hotel.

Louisa knew from experience that the hotel was haunted because a ghost in her room once got so active it moved her to the point of yelling, "You're scaring me, please leave." To which, the phantom responded immediately. She heard it run from the bathroom, out the door, slam the door shut and clamor down wooden stairs. When she opened her door, locked from the inside, she found the hallway had no stairs nearby and its floor was not wooden but covered in the Danieli's plush burgundy with green leafed carpet.

A tuxedoed waiter arrived at her table with a plate of delicate cheeses, switching her Danieli experience from haunted memories to lunchtime.

"Ahhh lunch," she toasted with her Murano-blown fluted wineglass, an homage to her anticipated visit to the island's municipal office and its ghost expert.

OTTO (8)

Ca' Foscari Clue

A writer from Murano named Roberto, an expert on Venetian ghosts, had been referred to Louisa by people at the municipality office. She knew of Roberto and had already written him about the ghosts. She'd mistakenly pretended she was asking about it for a Halloween party:

> Caro Roberto, I am interested in learning more ghosts on Murano. Where I can find in your book? We celebrate Halloween in American with pumpkin carvings and costume parties. I would like to include your traditions in my celebrations.

The ghost expert, Roberto, although polite, seemed somewhat insulted by this request:

Cara Louisa, I thought very much to your proposal, but I have to say, "No, thank you." I want to explain myself and my position: this year, in more than 100 places in Veneto will take place "*spettacoli di mistero*", a festival created using various kind of spectacles to give "voice" to several myths and legends of the places, exactly where they took life. Some stories risked seriously to be forgotten, and one of the reasons (not the only, but it helped), was the increase of Halloween parties, activities, events, that in the past 15 years took place in our society. The use of pumpkins is very ancient in our mountain communities, is used since centuries. We want to create a new conscience into young people, speaking of *Ognissanti* instead of that Halloween. We don't refuse it: everyone celebrates that night as he feels, but we cannot forget from where we come. So, it would be strange, for me, associate my name to an event to take place in Halloween contest. I'm sure you would agree with me. Sorry, not his time, not this event. *Grazie per la comprensione, Un abbraccio* (a hug), Roberto

Louisa replied as followed hoping to repair the damage from her first email:

Caro Roberto, You are so kind. Thank you for the history of *Ognissanti* and stories forgotten. I understand it is too important. Now I must tell you my true reason for contacting you. I am investigating for the police department and, I cannot say why I think this, you can help.

Have you any information that might help locate houses occupied by Nazis during the war that could be haunted?

His response, although cryptic, had led to the *Ca' Foscari* library where she found a book containing a clue, a piece of paper wrapped in red ribbon and folded into a hexagram shape.

When she unwrapped the paper, a poem was written in Venetian dialect, but for some reason, she could read it all. Another strange occurrence, she could only read the *Ca' Foscari* clue once. After that she couldn't understand the *Venexiano*. Too afraid to show it to a Venetian, she wrote out a translation from memory. Her memory of the poem was eerily perfect. It read:

At night is when we walk the grounds,
To find the places all around,
Were we live a sober life,
Free from watchful eyes and strife,
We wondrous Venice ghosts abound.
Beyond the sound of tolling bells
But not so far from Venice swells
Lies a ship of fishing fools,
Lies a ship's brass cutting tools,
There sits a plate with tails that tell

Louisa deduced that she would need to find the ship refer-enced in the clue. Probably she would have to scuba dive on it, explore it. To do that, she'd probably have to trust Matteo.

The last thing she wanted to do, trust Matteo.

༺◉༻

After her email correspondences with the ghost expert, she decided only to speak with him in person and not write anything else down. Before she met with him, she read all of his books about ghost legends, fantastic tales of haunted palaces and headless bodies or other fright-ening objects seen floating in canals or dancing inside abandoned buildings. Roberto documented, in a detailed fashion, many dark stories that Venetians had told and retold for decades.

Roberto wasn't happy about Louisa's questions but even-tually agreed to meet with her at his home. He told her to talk to a Burano fisherman named Bruno. Bruno could name every shipwreck in the lagoon.

Louisa didn't believe this was possible. She dove for years all over the world and treasure hunters continued to find new shipwrecks. The Venetian lagoon, although confined and shallow in spots, was also vast and remote. There was no way to tell how far out the shipwreck in the poem could be found. If it were off shore in the Adriatic sea, it could be sitting hundreds of feet deep. Even in the lagoon region, unknown islands, marshes and rivers existed that weren't on any maps. Burano, a tiny ancient fishing village at the far-thest reaches of the lagoon, was the next major island after Murano.

She decided to visit Bruno despite her doubts.

❦

The boat ride from Murano was uneventful. More than a few glass factory workers took the boat home after work to Burano, a fact not lost on Louisa. Nor did Louisa miss noticing that the Buranese were taller and stockier than most Venetians. Manlier men, perhaps?

Once there, she tracked down Bruno easily. The island was much smaller than Venice, so everyone knew him. When Bruno saw the poem Louisa held in her hands, he shook his head then his fists. He refused to drink the coffee she ordered for him and mumbled to others in the bar. The bartender pulled both coffee cups off the bar and motioned her out the door.

Alone and frightened, Louisa walked from the bar and tears swelled in her eyes. She'd not been shunned this way by any Venetian. Not even the meanest, jealous women from Venice, who felt her a threat to the handsome men, had treated Louisa as rudely.

An old woman in a fur hat and coat came to comfort her, told her not to cry and silently mouthed the word, *autiamo,* help us. She stroked Louisa's hand gently, looked into her eyes and again silently mouthed, *verde, verde, verde,* green, green, green. Louisa didn't understand but when she tried to repeat it, the women slapped a hand across her mouth and rapidly shook her head back and forth. Then she turned and hobbled away.

Louisa's hand burned where the woman had touched it. She swore she saw the word *verde* written there. She tucked her hand inside her coat to protect it.

On the ferry, a light rain must've washed the word off her hand. It disappeared.

❧

With no idea what the odd woman's words meant, she stopped at Murano Island on her way back to Venice. She decided to pay a return visit to the ghost expert and ask Roberto what *verde* could mean to the Buranese. She would not to tell him how they had mistreated her.

"Why do you ask about *Verde*?"

Not wanting to give anything away, she said nothing and simply shrugged. She couldn't risk another dismissal, this time by Roberto. Worse, she might evoke interest in him, for this new ghost story, and he might try to follow her.

"Where did you hear this word? It means green, that's all," he continued.

"I know it means green. What could green mean, specifically, to the Buranese?"

"Green," he repeated trying to read her face for clues to a secret he knew she held.

"Well," she paused. She'd planned this conversation on the ferry to Murano but in the presence of Roberto, the ghost expert, he became like the ghosts themselves. He seemed to take over all her plans and she found herself talking when she had promised herself to stay silent. "I, I," she stammered. *Hurry,* she told herself, *he knows you're stalling.*

"Ah, you must mean the island," he offered.

Damn. An island named *Verde*. He knew about it too.

"Don't worry, Louisa, I have no intention of going all the way out to Verde. I won't ask the little couple with the cantina any question about this note, this poem from your ghosts."

Apparently he knew everything about it. And had just told her everything she needed to know in one sentence. With emphasis on the phrases *all the way out* and then on the clue, *the little couple with the cantina.*

She laughed at her foolishness. "Roberto, if you knew the answers were on Verde Island, why did you send me to Burano?"

"I didn't know it," he said. "Not until I saw your face when you walked through the door. The Buranese scolded you. They're hiding something. Who told you about *Verde?*"

Louisa said nothing, which said everything to Roberto.

"Another ghost," he said, "or perhaps another interested party." Then he finished his coffee, walked to a cabinet and retrieved a bottle. "Grappa. The strongest I have. You're going to need it." This time the emphasis was on the word, "need."

After they each drank a small shot of grappa he'd poured for them, he said, "On second thought, take it with you. For the next time you visit Bruno, the Buranese."

"Grappa?"

"Grappa. If you get him a little drunk -- and only this strong stuff will work because he drinks every day, all day -- then he may soften to you."

Louisa knew it wasn't a second thought at all. It was the sole reason he retrieved the grappa. He didn't intend for her to get him a little drunk either. Nor did he want her to soften him. The grappa would get that Buranese drunk and passed out, plain and simple. She supposed he thought her plan for Bruno and the other Buranese could evolve from there.

He nodded as he saw her mind interpreting the grappa gesture. Then he nodded again as he held it up and looked her in the eyes.

He turned to tidy papers on his desk. He moved dishes from the table. He returned books to the shelves, all in a polite but obvious message that it was time for her to leave.

She responded appropriately, put on her coat and walked to the door.

"Go to Verde first," he said. "Take the poem. Bring a trustworthy translator. Trustworthy," he repeated. When he saw her mind working again he added, "Matteo cannot be trusted too often but, this time, he will have to do. Anyone else would be too risky."

"Why isn't Matteo risky," asked Louisa, "you know he's always drunk and crazy?" Of course she didn't ask Roberto how he knew Matteo. They both had once lived on the same tiny island, Murano, a fishbowl even smaller than Venice. She didn't ask how he knew that Matteo and her had been an item. He'd surely witnessed their street dramas of the past.

"Because he already knows what you are up to," replied Roberto. He seemed in a hurry for her to leave.

"He does? But h . . .," she began.

"Don't ask how Matteo knows," Roberto interrupted, "it is so."

He shuffled her out the door while adding, "Do not go back to Burano until you talk to the Verdenese. Investigate the clue exactly how the couple on Verde suggest." This time, it seemed to Louisa, he emphasized every word.

He'd packaged the grappa in burgundy tissue paper and tied it with gold ribbon. Before she departed, he took the neatly packaged grappa back and kissed it good-bye.

Or had he kissed it good-luck?

Once outside the door, she leaned towards his cheek to offer the customary air kisses, but he pushed his hand in front of her, refusing the gesture. He glanced around the *calle*, as if the neighbors watched their every move in the arched doorway of his home. They probably did.

He spoke softly, "Do not come back here. I am sorry."

"Can I . . ."

"No. No communication again. Ever," he pleaded.

For some reason, she knew exactly what he was trying to say next, without his saying a word. *I'm sorry to leave you in the hands of Matteo, but he is your only hope.* His apologetic face with furrowed brows and resolute frown, expressed a sad assuredness for her. He closed the door and Louisa heard a long series of clicks.

He'd locked, chained and double-bolted the door behind her.

✺

First, Louisa had to find the Jewish woman from Murano who knew about the Nazis. Louisa had learned that the strange woman grew up in Venice during the war and currently lived in Paris. The woman not only believed in ghosts but had clairvoyant powers of her own.

Louisa would meet with Matteo for the trip to Verde Island later. He'd know how to find "the little couple with the canteen." The trip to Verde might also invite another sexual spark between her and Matteo, but Verde and Matteo would have to wait.

For now, Paris was calling.

NOVE (9)

Tiffany Is Not Murano

"Paris is calling," the operator said to Barbara.

It was Louisa, calling collect. *Not from Venice,* thought Barbara.

During a beautiful breakfast at the Danieli, her tranquil fantasies of two Venetian admirers, Gianni-architetto and cafe owner-Seba, all screeched to a halt. They were replaced by an image of Louisa standing amongst gothic cathedrals with massive stain glass rose windows, surrounded by busy chocolate shops, long crunchy loaves of bread, outdoor cafes filled with scores of hyper, smoking people and an imposing Tour Eiffel looming over the bustling metropolis.

This shift in Louisa's center of activity jolted Barbara like a loud train whistle nearing its stop just as a morning commuter was about to enjoy a satisfying drag of a cigarette. The commuter is forced to stomp out the cigarette and Barbara stomped out the fantasy of her Venetian holiday with two men. She got on a mental train for her Parisien ride through Louisa's eyes.

How had Louisa materialized like magic in the City of Light? What was her crazy sister doing there? Louisa had said nothing of an intent to rush off to "gay *Paree*" within the next twenty-four hours.

Barbara wasn't surprised. Impetuous actions unfortunately were the norm for Louisa. Growing up near an Ohio steel town, the sisters slept in the same bed together for years and were more like twins than three years apart. Louisa -- her best friend, her only sibling, trusted servant and confident -- Barbara knew her well. She felt more like Louisa's mom, having to protect and defend the more impetuous one. Barbara covered up her misdeeds or fixed her dilemmas.

One night, while in their teens, Louisa climbed out the bedroom window to meet her boyfriend minutes before their stern father peeked in to check on his girls. According to plan, Barbara piled clothes under the covers of Louisa's side of the bed, waved to dad and whispered "She's out," implying Louisa was sleeping. If he checked under the covers, she could say, "I meant *she's outside*," but he never checked because her father trusted Barbara, the good sister. The good sister didn't lie, or so he thought.

Despite inner rebelliousness, both Louisa and Barbara resisted urges to break out of these roles. They stayed in the boxes the world assigned. Growing up working class and eager to make a life for themselves, leaving small town middle America became their primary concern--the fastest way out of the box. Thus, Louisa studied law and Barbara studied medicine and went to nursing school. Louisa had said, "I guess we both love a challenge."

And Paris, thought Barbara, *and glass*.

Louisa discovered her heightened passion for glass as a young adult, in the same place she felt heightened passion for so many other things -- aromatic wines, strong cheeses, coffee with steamed milk sipped while standing, vintage couture fashion and mind-boggling modern art. She found it all when she was in the pinnacle of passion -- where else? -- in Paris.

The first time Louisa gazed up, mesmerized by the moon reflected in the new addition to the Louvre, a pyramid of glass cleverly designed by Ming Pei, she knew she wanted to create things with glass. That was the thing about Louisa, she didn't just "visit" places. She immersed herself in every detail, like she did with Paris and the Louvre. Louisa studied the language and the art of Paris. She moved there for school, she lived it. She yearned for it.

To her, the Louvre glass pyramid was -- as she described it -- "perfect because it is perfectly wrong." Barbara understood what Louisa meant. Being the Louvre's self-reflecting sister, the glass pyramid remained unattached, a geometrical contrast to the exquisite lines of the Louvre Palace, a neoclassic jewel. So much was wrong with the pyramid's exacting straight steel that framed glass sheets and formed its point in the middle of a grand, elaborately decorated Parisen courtyard. The pyramid, as a stand alone, was loud not beautiful. Nonetheless it captured the beauty that surrounded with its modern window panes, their transparency and complexity made to reflect exquisite patterns off of the adjacent fountain and pool.

Both sisters marveled at how perfect in its contrasts was the Louvre's pyramid to its Palace. Such was the duality of this controversial glass structure, that even through Louisa's glazed, drunken eyes, the first time she saw it, she knew something had changed in her that very night. It happened immediately when she set foot in the City of Light. The Eiffel Tower twinkled, lovely lighted trees illuminated the *Champs Elysee* and the Louvre itself could be enjoyed by her all at once, so perfect was the placing of the pyramid.

If Louisa's true love of glass was first piqued by the glass pyramid then it was solidified at the Museum of Art Nouveau with the stained-glass objects created by Louise Confort Tiffany. *What is it about this work that penetrates my soul?* She caught her breath whenever she viewed Tiffany glass lamps, windows, statues.

This strong affinity with the artist changed Louisa's life completely after her encounter with his work in Paris such that she wondered if the ghost of Louis Tiffany dwelt within her. Why were her senses stirred by his graceful, useful objects of colorful and intricately pieced together glass? Was Louisa alive, in another form, in another life, during the art nouveau movement? Could that be why it all touched her deeply in the present? Perhaps she was a tailor in one of the fashion houses that adopted the Tiffany style. Perhaps she helped orchestrate the architectural renaissance of the form in New York, Chicago or Paris itself.

Here in Paris, she saw pieces in the artistic style that grew as a reaction to the harsh and rigid, geometric squares and rectangles of the industrial age (which oddly the Louvre Pyramid emulated) and her love of glass freely bloomed. The delicate lines, curvy plant stems and flower petals worked into glass, captivated her like no other works of art in the city, a city that not only exploded with all modes of art but also exploded with glass art, like that in the windows of the great cathedral of Saint Chappell.

Louisa Mangotti might've trained to be an attorney but she was an artist at heart. Gifted at birth with a talent for both, she struggled between extremes. Half Italian by descent from both her father's parents and German filling in the rest, Louisa's life and heritage contrasted itself like the modern and old buildings of the Louvre. It was strange, indeed perfectly wrong, that she chose Paris as her first European city to visit, instead of Venice, Rome, Florence or Capri, as her ancestry might otherwise demand. Yet, like many things in her bountiful life, Louisa's love of Paris began fortuitously, with a travel newsletter that alerted her to a last minute airfare sale. Her road to Tiffany and Paris was not filled with dreams of French food, or glass, or sidewalk cafes. Nor did history or nationality lead her there. Nor was love of art the catalyst.

What led her the first time to Tiffany was cheap airfare and an asterisk in a friend's guidebook.

Many years and adventures later, Louisa began to tell Barbara an odd tale, one that most would have found ridiculous. Having Louisa for a sibling, Barbara ceased to be surprised long ago by Louisa's stories. Dismayed, yes, but infrequently shocked.

While her Danieli waiters brought numerous double cappuccinos to Barbara, today she was both captivated and concerned during her phone call with Louisa and with what she heard about her sister's meeting with the Parisien courtesan.

It was already dark when Louisa woke late in the afternoon after an all-nighter in a Parisien cabaret and her evening of taking pictures of the monuments. Staying up all night suited not only Louisa but Paris, a city where illuminated tours abounded and restaurants didn't fill for dinner until eleven o'clock. Museums, including the Louvre, were brilliant at night in their stillness and lack of tourists. Late museum hours allowed Louisa to make her first museum-marathon years ago, some fifteen museums in three days.

Over the phone, Louisa explained to Barbara that a clerk at the Murano municipality had suggested she meet a woman in Paris who'd lived in Venice during the war. This Parisian woman, now known as Madame de Carlo, grew up near a haunted Murano house, or so Louisa had been told. De Carlo's current home, appropriately located on the Rue la belle Dame, sat on the left bank of the Seine River. From all accounts, De Carlo was a stunner as a young Jewish girl who used her beauty to her advantage and saved her own life posing as a Venetian during German occupation.

Louisa didn't know much about the woman when she arrived in Paris--just that she might possess information about the old home on Murano island, near the factory where the dead glassmakers had worked. In particular, she was said to be familiar with its ghosts, perhaps of the Nazis rumored to have lived there.

In her seventies, the woman, remained strikingly beautiful such that her anti-aging secret had kept her in tact for the business she plied since the war. "A high paid occupation" was all the Muranese ghost expert, Roberto, and the man at the municipality would say.

Madame had insisted they meet at a famously expensive restaurant and a waiter guided Louisa to a quiet secluded area. There sat the most intriguing creature, who'd outlined her striking, almost orange-colored eyes in what would have been too much liner on any less of a beauty. She'd painted her lips vibrant pink and wore gold dust upon batting lashes. Rose gold chandelier earrings swung to her shoulders and peeked from under thick, magenta-streaked black braids, which fronted a full head of hair and framed both breasts. Her bosom was propped up with a burgundy lace bra, which was revealed, not inappropriately but sultry, through a sheer white body hugging shawl. The only evidence Louisa could see of a blouse under the shawl were its embroidered sleeves and cuffs that hung too far (yet not too far) over delicate fingers. A different ring graced each finger, including her thumbs, one covered with a ruby and the other, a canary diamond. A very large diamond at that.

Louisa shook the woman's hand and noted interesting quirks. One eye twitched, her chin quivered, as though she were itching it or wanted to, and the enchanting Jewish-woman-turned-Venetian-now-French-courtesan was foaming at the brim with anxiety. Surrounded by gilded, framed paintings, in a dark booth piled with lush fabric pillows and enclosed in rich crushed velvet drapes, Madame De Carlo raised her eyes and her hand-blown glass flute, which held what looked like a Kir Royal cocktail, or Champagne with Chambord, before Louisa could squeeze in next to her. She pointed the glass at Louisa and said, "He never understood, never could, never tried, she was loose, or she was frigid, maybe too harsh to him." Then she raised her glass a bit more and winked at Louisa. Her eyes then fell to a paper and pen on the table beckoning Louisa to write it all down. Louisa picked them both up and started to write.

Was it a toast? A riddle? To agree to this meeting, the woman had ordered Louisa to bring a piece of Tiffany glass to her, which she now carried in its trademarked light blue packaging. Her phone conversation with Rianna de Carlo, as this woman called herself in the twenty-first century, had been filled with propositions, odd conditions, as though she wanted something, hinting things at whim as she barked curt and short orders.

"You bring glass, I bring myself, you listen," Rianna had directed Louisa on the phone.

After sipping some of her blush-colored cocktail from what Louisa presumed to be Tiffany crystal stemware, this strange and gorgeous woman continued her mock toast-poem with glass raised high, "He felt spasmodic, nervous spasms at the knees. She was sexy, she was plain, perhaps nasty, to him."

She winked, drank, slid across the burgundy leather seat and, with glass still in the air, patted next to her for Louisa to sit.

Louisa began to speak and the woman, without looking up from another Tiffany box that sat next to her on the small sofa, shushed her.

"Bring the glass, I bring myself, you listen, remember?" she said with eyes shifted now to the blue box beside Louisa.

When she did look up at Louisa, her head jerked back.

"Why did you bring him with you?" she said to Louisa who sat alone. "No, don't answer" the woman corrected herself. "You don't speak." she said and gestured for the Tiffany box Louisa had brought with her.

"Excuse me but I don't know why I am here or why I should give this to you?" Louisa said.

"Then leave," replied the woman. She drank again. After the drink, she reminded Louisa of a promise she was now breaking, "Bring the glass, I bring myself, you listen."

Holding her hand out again, she repeated, "Bring. The. Glass."

Louisa hesitated for a second, looked around her and froze. This was a scam. A Venetian scam. How? Why? Who? Ana? Roberto?

"Do you want me to get rid of your ghost?" Rianna asked with a lift of her head towards the air next to Louisa, "I'm not sure why he followed you here, this handsome American man."

Louisa laughed and thought, *You don't know with whom you are messing*?

"I'm not messing with you, Louisa, but your ghost is and he is very clever, led you to me. I suppose I must allow him to stay. I suppose," she said and toasted the air next to Louisa. "*Merci beaucoup*," she said to same spot, to a supposed invisible being.

"What does . . ." Louisa began but again the woman shushed her then slammed her fist onto the table, disrupting not only the silverware but several patrons nearby.

She curled her lip in disgust at the Tiffany box Louisa had set on the table.

The woman continued, calm, with her unusual toast. "He liked to have them easy, sweet, quiet, cute, not loud nor aggressive, opinionated or brute." She shook her head in approval of her toast and drank more of her Kir Royale.

"Okay, I will be nice," she said to the air next to Louisa. That is, to her ghost, not to Louisa.

She moved her head closer as if speaking some important information of which only she and Louisa were to be privy.

"Sitting pretty and shy, he could man-handle it. Because he wanted to possess her, would not let her get away. Or get her way. He told her 'no commitment' in every moment, every day."

Pleased with herself, she raised the glass high above their heads, pulled it to her lips with dramatic flare, finished her drink and placed it on the table with equal drama. After nodding at the air next to Louisa, she arranged her champagne flute more perfectly in front of her and twisted her head sideways to face Louisa head-on, "Now you may speak."

"Well, first, what was that about?"

"It was about the ghost."

"What ghost?"

"The one in Murano," she said with raised eyebrows to the air next to Louisa as if in agreement about something, something like "she really doesn't get it does she?"

"Who is the Murano ghost?" asked Louisa.

This question annoyed the woman very much and she replied in a tone that implied she thought Louisa was as dumb as rocks.

"The Nazi," the woman said, as if she would rather spit. As if she never wanted to ever have to say that word.

"What Nazi?" Louisa asked, almost apologetically.

This time, even more annoyed, Rianna replied slower, like she was speaking with a child, a very stupid one.

"It doesn't matter what Nazi. It is a Nazi. Don't go there." Each time she said the word "Nazi" she said it while blinking her eyes as if she was pleading with Louisa to not make her say it again.

When Louisa opened her mouth to speak, the woman stopped her, this time pleading, "They are filth. You have no idea the filth they spread. Do not go back to the Murano house. Ever."

All this questioning, travel to Paris and a 200 euro piece of Tiffany glass, for that information, thought Louisa. It was the cheapest piece of Tiffany glass she could find. All of it to find out she couldn't go back to the haunted Murano house.

The woman laid her hand on Louisa's hand and tapped it hard. It hurt.

"Yes. You are very cheap," she said. "200 Euro? I make that in fifteen minutes with the right Nazi," and this time it was final. She would never utter the word again in her lifetime.

Then she curled her lip again at the Tiffany box Louisa had set on the table.

"I will tell you this -- the people you mess with there are murderers. Greedy monsters. Let me finish talking, do not interrupt, like you seem to have occasion to do at your whim, Ms. Mangotti." she said. Then, nodding again at the air, added, "Don't worry. Despite how I may react to you, I love everything about your brazenness and courage," she waived at the waiter to refill both their glasses. At the thought of a ghost following her from Venice to Paris, which might now be sitting next to her, Louisa had emptied her glass as well.

The Parisien woman continued her diatribe waiving the empty flute.

"For she was like a virus, could be blown in the wind, and she, like a victim, would be punished if she sinned."

For a second, Louisa's thoughts drifted to Matteo, but when the woman instantly sensed it and scolded Louisa with her eyes. Louisa came back to the present. The woman emphasized the first word of the next sentence as if to say, *listen close.*

"Her eyes revealing, he had slowly touched, as though he were peeling off a shell so slim. He thought her appealing, plenty forceful not too much."

She gave Louisa another look of *don't let your mind drift away from my words.*

"She seemed a bit freewheeling, so he told her not enough, challenging adventure was not his game and so he idly waited for a lion more easily tamed. Although she was exciting, she was boring, not too intense. For him. She was sexy, she was fun, not too demanding for him."

What is all of this about, Louisa wondered, but only for a brief moment. Her mind went to Matteo. This sounded like her relationship with him, but the odd Parisian woman would not allow drifting thoughts for too long. *It must be a coincidence, the similarity of this woman's rantings to her experiences with Matteo.*

"Not a coincidence and not rantings. The truth," the women said and answered Louisa's thoughts. "I assume you were chosen for this reason: because he loves you, both Venetians love you. Perhaps you too will choose, one of them, someday. Not this trip," she said. First confiding then predicting, as an aside.

Louisa shifted nervously.

"As for my odd manner that you just reflected upon, you are odd too, Louisa. The na," she started to say something. Then she remembered her vow to herself to never say that word again. In her lifetime. "They didn't defile you, and then your sister, and then kill her. Like she was nothing more than a pesky insect."

Louisa knew not to say one word to that, so she rested her head back on the high cushion of red velvet and held her gaze straight ahead, in sympathy.

"Maybe now you don't feel so bad giving me this cheap piece of Tiffany for the priceless clue I am giving you." Before Louisa could say it, the woman said, "I know you don't understand my words. Yet." Next speaking directly to Louisa, not as a riddled toast, but as one confident and strong woman to another, she explained,

"The victims of the sorted crimes you ask about? They are like my sister. Helpless. You are not like her. You are not caged. You can find them. Help the caged ones. Please go now, all this talk has exhausted me." She waived at the waiter to give the check to Louisa, which he did.

Then the woman left the restaurant to "meet an old friend."

Louisa did not feel disappointment. What little she had learned was valuable. She now knew there were victims of crimes, plural. They were caged, docile and shy, like the woman's sister. The perpetrators were either Nazis or people associated with them. Louisa had written down as much of the woman's words as she could. The Parisien had encouraged her to write it down but also had not slowed down for it either. Her eyes had followed Louisa's note-taking and sped up in sync, her voice seeming to manage the note-taking so scribbles had resulted and only Louisa could decipher them. Later.

When Louisa got up to leave the restaurant, the waiter blocked her path. He pointed to the receipt for the drinks. She had paid the bill but had left the receipt. She shook her head to indicate that she didn't need the receipt.

"Madame?" He handed it to her.

"Your ghost said to read it," she thought she heard him say as she walked out the brass framed door.

In the quaint Parisian alley next to the cafe, she stopped to look at the receipt. A strange wind blew past her. It was pink, not foggy, but a very bright pink, like the Kir Royal cocktails.

"Help them," the wind seemed to whisper. On the receipt, a drawing of a Greek symbol topped the page and it also included directions for Louisa.

It directed her to Accademia museum and one of the most famous pieces of Venetian art.

DEICI (10)

Malfeasance of Matteo

Water is precious everywhere but in Venice, where it is the only thing that's free. Too free. Very unruly, Venetian water is not collected drop by drop like in Tuscan towns or Umbrian hillsides nor sacrificed unwittingly as on suburban golf courses or slope-side ski resorts. Neither is it hoarded, courted, siphoned nor saved. In Venice, water is wasted, wadded in, wished away then washed down countless drains. The lagoon that surrounds and supports the Venetians is muddled in a myriad of marshes. Tons of water tumbles today towards their homes and is tossed out tomorrow. Yet Venice thrives in it. How?

Hardly a soul could argue against the advantages of extra water: it clears the sinuses, refreshes the air, cleans the hair, presses wrinkles, fills the belly. But water in Venice is not benign. It can be vile, a cesspool. And why? Too much water.

Water, water, everywhere, and no drops to drink, thought Matteo. It made him sick. Matteo despised the lagoon as much as he loved it. His home, his prison. A proud Venetian sailor, Matteo grew up on and lived many lives on the water. Won rowing competitions, skillfully raced speed boats, found hidden places the lagoon offered like run-down abandoned buildings where he and his troupe could "make a party." He strolled its shores, played with its finest playmates. Even lived in his boat every time his father kicked him out of the house. Matteo needed the lagoon.

That's why he despised it. He hated needing it. He hated needing anything.

After his father, Guiseppe, threw him out a final time, he tried to force Matteo to work for a living and find a real home of his own. Papa took his boat, sold it to some scum. So Matteo ran away, no problem for him to run, to move to England, live on the streets for a time. Couldn't live on the streets in Venice or any other lagoon island without a boat.

He had moved to London, learned English and continued hustling. Why should he work in a factory or at a winery? He didn't need a job.

He had a job, a very lucrative one. He needed a boat. And he got one, he always got what he wanted. Now back in Venice, he worked the streets and that job gave him freedom. It gave him glamour, girls, supplies and no tax bill to force him to send money to the powerful Vatican. The Vatican had enough money and he had had enough of the Vatican. He had enough of those factory jobs. Matteo didn't need any grueling winemaker or glassmaker job. Long hours standing near ovens hotter than a desert tarmac, around the intense fire all day. For what? A paycheck? His pockets were always full of cash and that was good enough for him.

What did he want for? Nothing. Except for this fucking lagoon. The lagoon was like a woman, the worst kind. The kind he couldn't live with or without. One he needed. Like water, he both despised and loved women. In Matteo's heart, he didn't want an American girl nor did he yearn for a Venetian woman. He wanted a hostage. No, he didn't want a hostage, he needed one. Needed. *Pttt-tzoo,* he mockingly spit whenever he thought it.

He remembered meeting Louisa many years ago, right after he got out of rehab, his third time at age twenty. She was a little older, a brilliant student, a sexy young girl, full of energy, enthusiasm, electricity. He ruined her. He intended to ruin her. That's what he did, who he was, he didn't mean anything personal by it.

At first, he thought it could work, he could love her, he could stay clean. That part he was sincere about. He was forever sincere about that part. For a day, maybe a week. Maybe once or twice, at the longest, for a month. Usually it was a facade. The love, the attempts to stay clean, stay sober. He knew it was a facade. A sincere facade.

He became addicted to relapse. To playing the relapse game, short term sobriety with a stint in rehab every year to keep them all off his ass.

He played it very well during the three years he and Louisa were together, on and off, back and forth she went. That girl made him so miserable. She thought she was clever coming and going like she did. Playing her own little relapse game. It didn't work. Her game. How many girls came and went between her moves, her game? Many. Very many. It was easy. Sometimes too easy. It was a buffet. Venice is a buffet.

One time when he left rehab--one of several releases he orchestrated just when she thought it was safe to visit Venice again--he cried to her "I love you I need you I can't live without you."

It was true or it was false. Nothing was real to him during his time with her, and without her, when she went back home to America, as she always did, vanishing from him like a ghost. To him, she melted then formed again into another piece of work, a piece of art, like glass art.

Matteo perpetually knew she could leave him again. He trusted her to do that much. Free him for a while. Chain him with her absence, hold him in her own freedom, his jail. She wouldn't commit to him. Ever. He needed that commitment, the hostage to stay. He must move on with his life and have her with him here too. While he moved, she should stay. That was the plan.

"*Ma va fa culo,*" (fuck you). He screamed to the lagoon, partly to Louisa who sat behind him in the boat. Mostly he cursed himself because, *ti volio bene, Louisa* (I care for Louisa*).* He yelled out to the lagoon but inside his head he yelled at all the reasons she still penetrated his heart.

His boat bounced and bounced over waves, which made him smile at the memory of Louisa with him years ago, pregnant. He didn't want the baby for the same reason he didn't want her here now -- she couldn't commit. What would she have done if that baby had been born? Taken it to America? He did not let that happen. He sped the boat up that day and it bounced over the waves. He drove faster, as fast as he could over wakes from passing boats. He remembered how the water slammed against the boat against her growing uterus, up and down with it, years ago.

Louisa remembered it too. She cringed. She had lost the baby. The lagoon took it.

Aborta, aborta, aborta, abortiamo, he had yelled to her when she told him she was pregnant. As if it was his baby, his choice. He knew it wasn't his choice. It was her womb. Her egg. Her child. Maybe his sperm. He didn't mean any of it. Sad when she miscarried back then, he frowned at the memory.

Today Louisa knew better than to tell him to slow down as they road together to Verde Island. It would only incite him. Yet Louisa's not telling him to "slow down" had the same effect. He wanted to see how fast he needed to go to make her say it, to make him slow down.

Just like your drinking, she thought. *Go as fast as you think you can until I break.*

He slowed down and pointed to an old Venetian palace on a tiny island. A palace from their past. There were many palaces and other buildings from which to choose out in the lagoon, but the structure they loved the most was partially flooded when she saw it back then and she wanted to make it new again. The day they found it, he went to the top, stood on the terrace and started doing karate moves. In between moves, he would stop, motion dramatically across the terrace and pronounce "We will make a party here."

Waste. What a waste, she opined to herself. But she couldn't feel sorry for him anymore.

Graceful and sleek, Matteo was a gifted athlete. Whatever sport he tried, he excelled at it. Rowing with first-rate skill and strength, he led his crew to national championship. His skiing was fluid, his form in tune with the hill. Karate done with effortless expertise. Between the parties he made.

Today they traveled between Burano and Torcello, far across the Venetian lagoon. For most of this afternoon, they had circled many small islands because Matteo, lost and confused, wasn't willing to admit it. She didn't know where they were headed, only Matteo knew for sure, knew at least where he wanted to go.

In his mind they were traveling to Isla Verde, Green Island, and from his lengthy perusal of these far reaches of the lagoon, there were many that fit the name but none were Verde. He couldn't fucking find it. Finally he stopped at a picturesque spot where they could relax in the sun and he could think about finding the course to Verde.

Louisa tried to relax, sun herself, jump out for swims while Matteo passed out, swimming in the ecstasy of his only true loves -- alcohol, drugs and control. He could do anything drunk. Row, ski, make glass, make love, make a party. Anything.

Louisa had no idea back then that Matteo was high most of the time. She didn't know it now either.

Stupid girl, concluded Matteo, relieved.

Yesterday when Louisa asked him to take her to Verde Island, and to introduce her to the Verdenese couple making the cantina, he'd asked, "what you want with them?"

He knew her answer was a lie and he wanted to slap her. He was in trouble. She offered to pay him. He needed the money. He took her to Verde because he needed her. He felt trapped. He hated her. God, she was beautiful.

Pttt-tzoo, he spit.

Louisa regretted needing him to take her out to Verde Island, where ever in the world it was, but she wanted to ask the two Verdenesi some questions. The ghost expert suggested she tell Matteo that she found out about the island from ghost research she'd done. She and Matteo both pretended he believed her.

With Matteo being his usual uncooperative self, tension hung in the air. Why was he taking so long to get there? Why had he stopped to sun himself? In the middle of the lagoon, somewhere between Murano and Burano? Somewhere, but where?

Louisa tried to enjoy it, the sun, the sea air, the boat rocking on gentle waves. She tried to be "in the moment." It truly was extraordinary out here, somewhere. Way out in the lagoon, alone with birds resting on canal markers, enjoying nature and sea breezes.

During the stop, he briefly woke from his dazed existence, leaned on one elbow and saw the most incredible beauty before him, sunning topless, hair blowing in the wind, smile across her face, sunglasses pressing down on her pleasantly tan cheeks. He wanted to take her. He had to have her. He was so hard. Alcohol, pot, things, did that to him.

She'd let him hold her, kiss her, everything, back then.

Today he knew she wouldn't let him do nothing. She'd claim it was their past or his drinking. It was only their past that stopped her from loving him, he knew.

Pttt-tzoo, he fake spit again.

He disgusted her sometimes. He knew he was disgusting. The nausea was coming. The rush was ending. The rush. The nausea always followed the rush. Sometimes both at the same time. If you move you could vomit. So he couldn't move. He lay there as still as possible, one elbow propped up to take in her beauty and her naked breasts.

"You never move," he used to tell her when he wanted her to run with him and she refused. He called her names, lazy, a sloth. He chuckled at the irony. "You sleep like a cat," he would say.

It was true. Louisa couldn't and wouldn't deny it. It hurt anyway. His insults.

Slowly she turned toward him and saw him lying motionless in the boat, sadly knowing something was wrong with him. "God please, no, not again" she almost cried out.

Instead of begging the universe to make him better, not drunk and sick, she went to him. She moved to his side of the boat, careful not to rock it. She laid her hands on his chest and her body down beside him, held him, cradled him. He was sick, that's all. Sick. She prayed. Although she wasn't aware of it, she prayed with him.

"God please help this man," she prayed with tears forming in her eyes as he too asked the universe for help.

"How can I help you baby?" she said quietly feeling his hardness on her everywhere.

"Help me?" he said surprised, not in a mean tone, more pathetically. "You can't even help yourself." He knew he needed help and that she could do everything for him.

She ignored his words and experienced the warmth of his body. They lay there together. Still. His hard body and penis pressed against her.

It didn't take long for Matteo to become overwhelmed by Louisa's kindness, her sweetness.

What a wonderful woman, why I do this to her?

Louisa too became overwhelmed by the strong passion she felt. Immediately it thrust upon her, him. She tried but failed to stop him from tearing her apart with his body. He kissed every part of her, her head, neck, navel. He breathed into her navel and ran his lips over her belly then went below it. Passion was as strong as the fear.

Fear.

Suddenly he stopped. He got up and vomited. Then threw her blouse at her and she put it back on. It was over. He wouldn't penetrate her. He did not want her to take their baby, his baby, to America. Louisa was his baby.

Fear. Louisa couldn't think straight. Aroused by him and the scenery, she'd ignored her own good sense and almost went too far with him. He had stopped it and that made her want him more. Nothing could turn her off. Nothing. Nothing. Nothing.

"We go," he said as if it was all his idea, as if he wanted to stop. It wasn't his idea at all. He didn't want to stop. He wanted Louisa to never leave him. Ever. He loved her. He needed a drink. Not of fucking water.

Oh well who cares if he thinks he interrupted what I wasn't going to stop. Let him think it. Louisa realized, in just that second, she knew she no longer loved Matteo. She merely lusted for him. Lusted, lusted, lusted.

For Matteo, unfortunately, it was the other way around.

"*Ma va fa culo,*" Matteo muttered. He flicked his hands in the air with a glance at her quickly. *She's my baby and I love her. She fucking knows it. She always knew it.*

"Where the fuck I am?" he asked her. "*Cazzo,*" (fuck), he said and laughed.

She loved his laugh, it made the lust stronger. Stronger. Stronger.

"Can we circle those islands over there again?" She pointed to a small group filled with trees and birds. She realized why they had stopped. Not only did he need to pass out, he was lost. If Matteo didn't get booze, and who knows what else, he was going to get mean, fast, like a mad blaze.

Frightened, she tried to sweeten her voice, "Can we try?"

"Oh you know fucking what? You know too much. You know Venice better than a Venetian? *Ma va fa.*"

Louisa wasn't going to fight this fight anymore. Not his drunk attitude. Nor would she argue that she often knew more about the lagoon than did some Venetians. Although she didn't live it like they did, she'd studied, observed, examined it. She knew Venice.

We have to get to that cantina and get this man some booze or I am toast no matter how much he loves me.

Begrudgingly Matteo did what she suggested. Soon he pulled into a long canal. On a short dock, they saw a couple, perhaps in their fifties, waving gleefully at the sight of their charming friend, Matteo.

And his inquisitive American girlfriend.

"*Mi amoroso,*" Matteo introduced her as his girlfriend. He knew Louisa understood him but didn't care. *The bitch is my girlfriend whether she wants to be or not. She is mine.*

Louisa prayed as she hurried off the boat, *booze, booze get this man some booze*. As she scrambled off the wobbly dock, her shoes sunk into muddy shores.

Tromping towards the eagerly awaiting couple, Louisa eyed large barrels, filled with what she assumed was wine, next to their tiny dock. The man Matteo introduced as Guido motioned him over to a lawn mower, apparently broken, so they attempted to start it.

The woman, Caterina, pulled Louisa away from the two men.

Caterina took Louisa over to the furthest point from the men. There Caterina showed her a small garden, no more than ten feet by ten feet, where she grew food. She guided Louisa down each row, pointed at plants in various stages of growth and proudly announced each specie in proper Italian, not dialect.

"*Melanzane,*" (eggplant) she said, her voice rose up at the end of the last syllable, for emphasis and acknowledgment, as if asking Louisa, "You know what that is right?" The garden tour continued in a charmed and intimate manner.

"*Pomodorini,*" she said, pointing first to the little tomatoes, or cherry tomatoes as Americans refer to them. "*Il carciofo.*" (the artichoke.)

But she said one artichoke, singular not plural.

"*Il carciofo, non i carciofi?*" Louisa asked for clarification. One artichoke, not artichokes?

Her garden guide replied by shaking her head back and forth. With a *Tsk tsk* and puckered lips, she held her arms out and shrugged her shoulders.

"No lo so perche. Troppo difficile," (I don't know why there is only one. They are too difficult.) Louisa nodded and gave her a sympathetic smile.

"Per me." Difficult for me, she said, laughed, then added, *"Ma provo."* But I try. She tried to grow artichokes but only produced one.

Caterina continued her garden tour and language class by pointing out more vegetables like *"le carrote,"* (the carrots) and *le patate* (the potatoes).

After she called out the potatoes, she took her right hand, pressed her finger tips together, kissed them and waved the closed fingers to the sky.

"Buona e brava," she said. Very good and very behaved. She started counting them, five at a time. There were nearly one hundred potatoes in the small plot. Louisa assumed they'd been planted in levels, stacked on top one another, although she couldn't be sure. How on earth could so many potatoes be planted in such a tiny area?

The women sensed her confusion, leaned down to see into her eyes and said, *"Non molto difficili. Le patate sono facili.* Not difficult. Potatoes are easy. *"E buone."* And good.

Next they went into the lettuce row, where the crops were noted, *"per insalade verde."* She rambled off the greens including several luscious stalks and varieties of radicchio, a favorite salad ingredient of the Veneto region.

Louisa didn't care for radicchio, it being too bitter for her. Every time she admitted this to someone who lived in the region, they looked at her as if she had just said, "I want to kill a lamb."

"What? You don't like radicchio?" they all said. She kept silent about it to Caterina who beamed with pride at her array.

Some other delicious salad ingredients grown by Caterina included *ruccola* (arugala), *le bietola* (mangold), and *la lettuga* (garden lettuce.) Caterina also grew *i pepericini, i cipollini, il porro, il cetriolo*--peppers, scallions, leek, cucumber.

Of course no Venetian vegetable garden would be complete without *i finocchi,* fennel, a common pleasing ingredient in many Italian meals. Caterina had plenty of it.

Louisa assumed the tour was over and they would be heading next to the cantina, which the owners had immediately announced to Matteo was complete when they exited the boat.

Caterina motioned her instead to the rear of a structure that Louisa believed was their home. There before her in all of its glory was the most stunning strawberry garden. Louisa shook her head at how this woman could possibly have kept or even started a garden in the dead of winter, just as she'd been amazed in Rome to see citrus trees sprouting lemons, limes and oranges in late December.

Caterina presented the strawberry garden to her with a sweep of it using both arms and a curtain call bow. *Fragolini.* Little strawberries. Louisa, shocked, couldn't help but show her disbelief to which Caterina confirmed it.

"*Si, i fragolini, assolutemente, si.*" Caterina began foraging through her crop, which obviously wouldn't be ready until May.

Louisa remembered going to the lake district outside Rome where the incredibly sweet but miniature strawberries grew in the wild. It took rare soil along the lakes and the perfect climate to produce them there. People came from all over the world during harvesting season to purchase these tiny strawberries and no one bought just one box. Louisa could eat a whole box in a matter of minutes. In May, Roman lake cities put *fragolini* into everything -- liquors, tarts, cakes -- although rarely a jam could be seen made of them. They were just too precious.

Now here in this remote little piece of marsh out in the middle of nowhere in the Venetian lagoon, Caterina, the Verdenese, had managed to cultivate them. Caterina observed Louisa's face, trying to imagine what she was thinking, and she imagined it perfectly.

When Louisa finally looked up, their eyes met, and with a broad smile, Caterina said, *"Incredibile, no?"*

"Si, si, si," was all the practically speechless Louisa could say. Foraging paid off for both of them for Caterina and Louisa had found two small strawberries almost ripe, one for each.

"Mangia," (You eat) said Caterina as she gleamed and handed one to Louisa.

Louisa, touched by Caterina's persistence in finding a strawberry for her to eat from the meager patch, closed her eyes and dropped it ever so lovingly on her tongue.

Thus, the little berry forged a bond between two women of different ages, cultures and languages, instantly, next to a fertile piece of dirt.

♋☉☋

Matteo and company tried starting the allegedly broken lawn mower. Louisa suspected they were chatting about another matter, a more sinister one. The mower miraculously began to work perfect. She heard the growl of its engine synchronized suspiciously with the end of her strawberry patch tour.

They were building a cantina, a bar. Priorities as usual. Barely had a roof over there heads or place to sleep way out there on Verde Island. Yet they had built a sizable cantina and created an impressive vegetable garden. Food and booze, rain or shine.

She hoped to have a chance to speak with the Verdenese couple about the clues she held in her possession but hadn't told Matteo about them yet -- a poem and a drawing. The poem she found in a book at the *Ca' Foscari* law library. Buried behind a shelf, a folded piece of paper had been right where the ghost expert had told her to go. She pulled out the poem to show Matteo along with a copy of the drawing that appeared on the receipt from her lunch with Madame De Carlo. It looked like a picture of fish but she wasn't sure. Possibly some animal from a Greek fresco or a fragment of a Pompei wall. *What is that?* She pondered it again.

Matteo, drunk or not, was clever and quick. He glanced at the drawing she held and without looking away from his wine glass, said, *"Delfino. Bello."* He nodded, approving its beauty.

A dolphin, thought Louisa, *of course.*

"*Si, si, delfino. Greco. Molto bello. Mi piace,*" he commented on the beauty and confirmed the Greek origin of the drawing while still not moving his eyes away from the wine he swished around in the hand-blown wine glass the Verdese insisted he use to drink it from, stupidly Louisa felt. He held the delicate glass up to the light before drinking the wine with his pinky finger out, Italian style.

Then again, thought Louisa, *he can steal replacements from his family's chest for those expensive glasses he will inevitably break when he gets more drunk.*

"Why you have it?" he said. She knew he spoke this in English because he didn't want the Verdenese couple to understand him.

Louisa did not respond. She got up and asked Caterina for directions to the bathroom.

"No, no," he said to Louisa. "*No va bene,*" he shook his head and finger at her. He tried to grab the sheet of paper but missed. He laughed and looked at her as if to say, "You can trust me. You must."

Louisa sat back down then calmly handed both clues to him after remembering the words of Muranese ghost expert, Roberto, again, who had told her in confidence: "*Matteo cannot usually be trusted but this time he will have to do. Anyone else will be too risky.*"

Next she pulled out her English version of the *Ca' Foscari* clue to review it. Matteo read the Venetian version that she'd written, while he drank the home made Verde wine and somehow also nibbled on pastries.

Caterina offered them some of the best and freshest Carnival *frittelle* Louisa had ever tasted. Of course, she'd tasted plenty of the little fried dough balls. These *frittelle* were filled with Nutella. Her favorite.

The poem confused Louisa in its simplicity and it overwhelmed her with its ambiguity. She peeked over at Matteo, who looked not the least bit perplexed by it. He bent his head slightly at her, a signal she interpreted correctly as "leave me with it for a bit."

Because she continued to stare at him, he glanced sideways at her and with his eyes gave her another reassuring nod. "We are a team, don't worry," his eyes told her, not at all bossy or with his usual gamesmanship. They were partners now. He meant business. He was serious. Although he didn't put the wine down. Ever.

She read the English version while Matteo read the Venetian:

> At night is when we walk the grounds,
> To find the places all around,
> Were we live a sober life,
> Free from watchful eyes and strife,
> We wondrous Venice ghosts abound.
> Beyond the sound of tolling bells,
> Not so far from Venice swells,
> Lies a ship of fishing fools,
> Lies a ship's brass cutting tools,
> There sits a plate with tails that tell.
> The story is an ugly one
> The story that is far from done.

Days after she met with the Murano ghost expert, there she was with her only two clues, both now in the hands of

Matteo. With one of his muscular arms draped over her shoulder, he raised a full glass of red wine with the other.

"Drink," he cheerfully said to the Verde couple, then turned to her and demanded, "not you. You drink too much." He guzzled his own wine like he was suntanning on the beach with a refreshing cola, smacked his lips, smirked and leaned to kiss her.

She pulled away but then thought better and let him. She was in this with Matteo now, whether she liked it or not. She liked it, whether she wanted to admit it or not.

He liked it too. He wanted to show it. He nodded at the piece of paper with the *Ca' Foscari* clue, which he held in the hand draped over her shoulder. He raised his eyebrows at her and smiled that gorgeous grin.

Louisa knew in that instant he'd figured out the poem's riddle. She also knew he would expect to be rewarded accordingly.

She would reward him, she would like it and she would show him that she liked it.

UNDICI (11)

Phantom Man

H er pants felt looser than when she arrived, even with
evening hot chocolate, morning Nutella crepes and
daily fare of pizza or pasta.

This trudging over bridges is working, Barbara thought.
She soon knew why.

The walk, seemingly not as long as the day she arrived,
jet-lagged and sleep deprived, still dragged on from her
hotel to the nearest public boat dock. She was getting good
at trudging. She pulled suitcases behind her over irregular
walkways, stopped at each bridge to grab handles before she
lifted them slightly and climbed the steps. At the top of each
bridge, she twirled the bags around to push them down the
steps then twisted them back behind her again to lug to the
next bridge. Seamlessly she repeated the process between

and on bridges and their numerous steps. Up and down, over and over, until she reached the boat launch after a number of bridges she cared not to count.

She wedged both suitcases into a corner of the *vaporetto* where she could enjoy the views, smell sea foam and read a book -- all while sitting outside in the sun on the boat. She also remained out of the fray of chaotic passengers, who formed crushing lines on either sides of her, depending on which side of the Grand Canal the boat stopped to pick up and drop off more people.

Barbara ignored the perusal and disparaging glares of what she instantly recognized as French or German tourists who hoped to intimidate her into giving up some of her choice boat deck real estate. Not a chance. *I may be American and usually polite but this isn't the United States. I'm onto your games, Europeans don't que, they push.*

She stared back at them, refusing to move until they decided that she was either also a European tourist or a Venetian hauling suitcases for holiday on the mainland. They relented and moved away from Barbara's side. She, victorious. They, surrendered.

By the end of her boat ride, she could tell the nationality of a person from the simple purse of their lips when they spoke. An actor might study it -- certain languages push the mouth in different ways. There were other signs as well. Germans and Americans were usually tall, had hips, breasts, broad bodies. *And French women are 'this' big,* Barbara thought, mentally holding up her baby finger.

Brits, for the most part, laugh and joke, at least when they are on their Venetian holidays. Nordics sport rosy cheeks and stocking caps. Italians, with either jet black hair or golden ringlets, walk with confidence and flair then pose if they see someone watch or stare. Equally confident in their Latin sex appeal and fashion as any Italian, the French carried themselves with a different poise, a more feminine one, with wispy bodies and flowing scarves, while Italians wore jewelry and sunglasses. Thus, tourists who ride the Venetian boats effect the varied climates of their homelands, pondered Barbara. She silently apologized to them all for her silly generalizations but justified them because she was a mutt and a seer--that is, a mixed breed as well as an intuitive who could move her mind within the nuances. *And here comes a jovial bunch of Brits. Cheers.*

As the Brits entered the boat, Barbara looked up and saw Piazza San Marco in all her glory, spread out for the shutterbugs who rushed to its side of the boat such that the weight shift heaved the vessel. With one glance at San Marco, she, instantly in love, anticipated her turn to disembark into the world of turning, narrow passageways. This fine city had returned to her good graces.

At times Venice could seem like a coquettish nymph, fancying the attention of every passerby while reservedly bearing her centuries old rising and falling waters. But her beauty is not a subtle one. Tired Barbara wanted to plop down her suitcase and nap. Nonetheless, she planned to put on her rambling attire and go forth in search of some Venetian mystery.

She'd need to go to *Campo Santa Marguerita* where the language school was located and mingle with whomever she found. *Voila! Prego!* Her mind began to bounce between languages, from *voila* to *prego* or *pronto* and plain old "bye-bye." Or as an Italian would say, "By-eee by-eee" just as they would say, "Okaaayee-ee." Ending their words an octave higher than would be spoken in English.

Language school, a necessity. Domani mattina, tomorrow morning, she concluded.

Barbara managed to walk the long stretch from the lingerie shop near Rialto bridge and over it to the lively fish and vegetable market on the other side of the Grand Canal. Along the way, she spied a compelling reason not to travel alone. Two attractive young woman joined together -- one sported a short black bob, the other, straight and long blonde hair -- and both wearing jeans in such a way that it would make lessor mortals shutter. But the most important part? They were holding hands, not like friends but as lovers.

This display of girl-on-girl affection, minimal as it were, had the effect of stopping the human traffic. Barbara couldn't understand how mere hand-holding befuddled her -- and others judging by the stares. One worker, who carried a bag of cement above his head, did a complete one-eighty turn when the hand-holding girls passed him.

Normally any form of stopping traffic, foot traffic that is, would be severely frowned upon. Traffic stopping usually resulted from a tourist ogling a common Venetian, but uncommonly elegant, sight. Or from a visitor stopped in the middle of the lane fiddling with a mostly useless map, or posing for photos or lingering too long on a bridge where gondolas floated underneath.

This was different. This was sexy. A line began to form behind the girls. Like the pied-pipers they were, they led the masses, some onlookers even ran to get in front of them for a closer look. People, men and women, moved as fast as they could to keep up with the lipstick lesbian couple. Why? To see if this was real or imagined? If these girls weren't ancestors of the infamous Venetian courtesans who displayed their breasts on *Ponte de le Tette* (bridge of tits), they certainly could be major competition, to which everyone seemed to be saying *brava* (well done). No fancy lace stockings, no lingerie, no push-up bras or bare chest exposing corsets -- just a single flaunting of a girlfriend by a girlfriend.

Barbara filed this practical information for women traveling in Venice, or perhaps anywhere in the Mediterranean. The power of the lesbian look.

After a quick regroup, Barbara floated down the Grand Canal again and nearly fell asleep from the boat's gentle rocking. Not every *vaporetto* that travels down the Grand Canal stops at every stop and this one passed hers en route to Louisa's apartment forcing her to disembark at *Accademia*, the great Venetian art museum located near the old wooden bridge of the same name. At least she'd be on the correct side of the hundred steps of the *Accademia* bridge when she began her route through the labyrinth that was Venice.

Missing a stop or getting on the wrong boat occurred often in this town and it could either frustrate or amuse, depending upon the mood. Barbara could accept her fate and enjoy the extra walk, viewing dramas and sights along the way or she could push and rush, passing scores of mindlessly strolling tourists who got in her way.

Today she chose enjoyment and amusement. The sun was out, Venetians laughed and sang in the streets and she really had nowhere to go nor any place to be. She'd been fruitlessly searching for her sister, who had not answered her phone calls for hours. When she last spoke with Louisa, she said she was following the trail of a well-documented *Ca'Dario* ghost story but Barbara knew Matteo was also back in her sister's life. Matteo, the dark, intelligent and wealthy Venetian, had turned out to too good to be true to her sister. Along with the ghosts, charismatic Matteo was another of Louisa's obsessions. It all preoccupied Barbara's mind such that any man near her might as well have been a ghost, a fog or a mist.

Louisa had said that Matteo asked her to meet him at the usual spot centrally located for meetings, *San Bortolo,* Venetian for Saint Bartholomew. *Campo San Bortolo* was west of the Rialto bridge and it held a big statue of the saint of the same name. Barbara chose not to join Louisa in *San Bortolo* because she would soon be sick enough of jumping and running to *San Bortolo* every time a Venetian wanted to meet up.

Barbara was also surprised Louisa had gone because she'd sworn off Matteo. Again. Perhaps it was part of Louisa's search for clues surrounding his knowledge of the ghost legends. Barbara tried to ignore ominous thoughts and bring her mind back to the path she was on, which hours of meditation had trained her to do. If she didn't pay attention, she might get lost on the way to the apartment and if she asked for directions the response would be the same. Venetians would say, with a hand pointing up the Grand Canal, *"alora, un ponte, un ponte, un altro ponte e sempre diretto."* (A bridge, a bridge, another bridge and always direct.)

Sempre diretto? Always direct? No way. Nothing is 'direct' in this town, Barbara had thought the first time she heard the direction to go "always direct." She'd laugh, shrug, then secretly curse the Venetian who gave this instruction. *How can anything be direct in these mazes,* she'd thought at the time. Later she realized that, although the streets aren't straight in Venice, most routes can be negotiated *directly* along the curve of the Grand Canal, the large river that splits Venice in half. They are two different words, *direct* and *straight*. Walkways might abruptly dead end, cross many bridges, twist and wind, but if she stayed always direct along the Grand Canal she would continue to move forward. Always. Direct.

Her thoughts meandered like the Venetian walkways but were suddenly interrupted by a sexy accent. A tall Venetian man smiled down at her.

"Ciao cara," (Hello dear) he whispered.

The enjoyment and amusement Barbara could find by missing her boat stop had just appeared to her out of nowhere.

"Ciao," she said, dropping her eyes but not before meeting his and scanning across his tailored jacket and fitted jeans.

"Sono persi?" (Are you lost) he asked. But he knew. They always knew. Venetian men could easily spot an obviously American woman lost in Venice.

Sempre pronto, (Always ready) thought Barbara. Louisa liked to say it about *Veneziani* (Venetian men), they are "always ready." *Always ready* to spot an American female alone, lost. *Always ready* in every way a girl could want or would need.

"*Tu sei un fantasma*?" Are you a ghost? she replied. Perturbed by Louisa's recent disappearance and annoyed by talk of ghosts wandering the city posing as gorgeous Venetian men, she simply decided to ask him.

"*Cosa*," (What?) he responded, concerned that she might be crazy, but at the same time delighted by the idea that she might be crazy. A crazy American woman could mean plenty of good fun for this Venetian.

"*E niente*," (It's nothing) she said.

"*Dimmi tutto*," (Tell me everything) he said sweetly. Interesting. An American female who had engaged him in conversation and a mysterious one at that. What he really meant was "*tell me everything about this idea that you think I might be a ghost.*" Or he meant to infer, "*tell me everything about how you find me so interesting that just by looking at me you actually asked if I were a ghost.*" These Venetian men were predictably curious.

Although Barbara was concerned about her sister's whereabouts, Louisa had done this before. She'd done this for as long as Barbara could remember. She disappeared like a ghost herself. During road trips with friends, everyone joked that they ought to put a harness on Louisa to insure her presence in the car for the long ride back home. If she didn't return for Happy Hour each day, she was either kidnapped or in love.

Both kidnapping and love were a possibility here. Yet despite its shadowy appearance, Venice is remarkably safe.

The problem was not with Venice but with Louisa's choice of company. She wasn't answering her Italian cell phone, which could be attributed to the left-behind phone charger in her apartment. It was disconcerting nonetheless.

In the middle of this reflection upon Louisa's either voluntary or involuntary retreat, Barbara realized inquiring eyes were on her. The distinguished, good-looking Venetian gazed down at her again. He seemed to be wondering when her attention would come back to him, where he believed it rightly belonged.

"*Cara,*" (dear one) he said in the sing-songy way that only an Italian (well, maybe a Frenchman) could say it. "*Dove sei,*" (Where are you?) he asked.

Given her internal conflict between attraction to him and distraction about Louisa, Barbara smiled the biggest smile at him that she could muster.

Inwardly she cringed. *What a ridiculously selfish time for her to disappear on me, right before I meet this handsome stranger.* It was possible that Louisa returned to the apartment by now and if confronted would say innocently, "What? What's all the fuss about?" Barbara hated that about Louisa.

This beautiful man stood before her, eager to please, and Barbara, very eager to be pleased, could only say, *Mi dispiace, mi sono occupato oggi.* I am sorry, I am busy today.

She wanted to say the more precise word, preoccupato, like the English word "preoccupied" which is what she really was. Latin languages are like that. Meaning one thing but sounding like another, which oddly is kind of what they are saying: *I'm preoccupied with someone or something els, in other words 'worried.'*

By now her new admirer, having not been paid enough attention (which to him meant rejection) reluctantly moved on to the nearest cafe, but not without first slipping his name and phone number into her hand. He pretended to kiss her good-bye, otherwise known as the air kiss.

Ah the air kiss, thought Barbara, *you don't even have to kiss me, the fake kiss did the trick. For now.* She sighed.

She looked at the paper he had slipped into her hand and read his name while walking. She said to him mentally, *Massimo, I hope to inadvertently, on purpose, see you here the next time I miss my boat stop.*

For she was sure that, like most Venetians, he frequented the same cafe, every day.

❧

She turned and saw that during her fantasy of Massimo, she'd walked straight and direct to find Louisa's apartment.

There they were, Louisa and Matteo, in the familiar embrace of a Venetian man displaying his charms to a hopeless female.

Barbara's relief at seeing the reappearance of Louisa felt considerably lessened by the appearance of Matteo. Disheveled and unkempt, he was either drunk or running away from someone or something, probably both.

Barbara gave Louisa her best, disgusted, *'What is he doing here'* look.

Louisa didn't ignore it, but pretended to ignore it and pulled Matteo closer to her and further away from Barbara.

It was painful, looking at the two of them together.

Matteo, who grew up in this strange lagoon town from a family with too much wealth and status, first ran small scams, graduated to petty thievery and eventually became a full-time gangster, complete with stolen Venetian antiquities, shoot outs and drug deals. A master-manipulator, Barbara sometimes wondered if Matteo could teach it. Perhaps he did. She'd watched his manipulative skill, but didn't understand a word of his wild and animated rants in dialect when he communicated with his Venetian friends. A born leader, Matteo seemed to lead himself and others down the wrong path his entire life. He showed no signs of stopping his wrong-turn journey anytime in the near or distant future. Not when it worked for him.

Barbara took a final look at the Louisa and Matteo scene. He was doing it again, performing some story for Louisa with graceful sweeps of the arms, regal nods of the head, dancing eyes and glistening mischievous grin. A skillful actor, gorgeous and gifted, even the strong, intelligent Louisa didn't stand a chance against his persuasion.

Barbara turned the last of the keys into one of several locks familiar to these huge Venetian woods doors, and left them alone. It was not the time to talk about the events of the past two days or her anger towards Louisa's lack of regard for anyone else. Barbara needed time to recover from her conflicted feelings of lust for Massimo and rage at Matteo. Louisa would tell her everything anyway, in due time, as she always did.

Here they go again, thought Barbara as she left the final scene of the two lovers.

❧

Once inside the apartment, Barbara glared at the offending left-behind phone charger and wondered if she still had time to catch Massimo at the nearby cafe.

DODICI (12)

𝔉ashion and 𝔉antasy

Courteous Italians greet all salespersons with "*buon giorno*" (hello) when they walk into establishments. It is considered rude to do otherwise. Louisa greeted them all too, which was the opposite of her custom in America, where employees welcomed her, not the other way around.

In the high-end fashion boutique on *Calle Marzo XXII* near San Marco, Louisa held up a black Versace handbag for Barbara to admire. She saw a vacant look and sneaky smile on her sister face.

"Nobody kisses as passionately as Matteo," said Louisa. She glanced at her sister to note her response. She didn't get one, so she added with a poke of the elbow, "Not even your two boy toys. Combined."

That's not possible, argued Barbara to herself. Then she commented on the Versace bag. "It feels of quality for sure. I really like the metal hardware. Clever the way it's placed."

"Come on," begged Louisa. "The dirt. I want the dirt on your three-way. You owe me." Barbara had told her about meeting two Venetians her first night in town and how they fought over her, but she'd said little else about it.

Barbara picked up another handbag, placed it on her shoulders and turned to Louisa, "I like this one better for me, don't you?"

"Why won't you tell me?" Louisa persisted while shaking her head "yes" to the handbag.

"I'm a little embarrassed by it. Two men? It's not like me. To be so free."

"It is now." Louisa concluded, having no idea yet how much truth was in her statement.

"See, that's what I mean. The implication that my little Venetian kiss competition makes me different, more loose. It didn't feel sleazy when it happened." *No it felt frisky, flowing, forward, festive.* "But when I talk about it I feel ...."

"Like a slut?" Louisa filled in the blank, having since moved from handbags to lingerie and was holding up a lacy pair of thigh high silk stockings. "There is nothing sleazy easy about some sensual kisses with two handsome, attentive men. A zipless fuck."

"Does it count as zipless if actual flesh was touched?" Barbara inquired, knowing the answer.

"Probably not," confirmed Louisa. *But if nothing was unzipped?* she wondered. She recalled her own zipless meeting with the Prada wearing man, Massimo. Then Louisa slipped into the dressing room with an armful of clothes unaware that Barbara had recently had her own encounters with Massimo, the second one being just last night.

❧

While she waited outside the dressing room, Barbara's mind drifted back to her second encounter with Massimo.

"Massimo," Barbara remembered she had told him, "I hope you know my sister is vulnerable and otherwise involved."

"Your sister is a very beautiful, intelligent and intriguing woman." Barbara recalled how her heart fell to her feet when he'd said it. "My interest in her," he continued, "is only professional."

"You mean to help you with the case?"

"No, I have the answer to the case."

"You know who killed the dead glassmakers?"

"I knew it before it happened, but it was not possible to prevent it."

"Why not?"

"Why not? Because you follow the people but when you don't watch, maybe when you sleep, it happens." His black eyelashes cast shadows over his eyes and created the impression they were a darker blue than turquoise, as they were when light shone into them.

Barbara had had a hard time concentrating on the important discussion. While he spoke of the case, her mind pictured him dressed in a blue brocade 17th century Venetian costume. Her mind's eye saw him wearing trousers that pulled into blacks bows at the knees with the same black satin tied into bows atop his courtly shoes. She imagined the ruffled front of his shirt flowing over his waist, no longer tucked in for he was already undressing, yet his long curls were still pulled back in their own black satin bow.

"Before you go too far in that fantasy, I must warn you, I see it in your mind," he had said.

She'd blushed. "You mean I'm that obvious."

"Obvious?" he asked.

She recalled how she tried to think of another word to explain what she meant by "obvious" like a word that more closely resembled a word in Italian. "Transparent," she'd corrected.

"Ah, transparent. No, you are not transparent but your mind is and I can listen to this fantasy and I can see it very clear. The costumes. But I don't see inside of you. I see what your mind sees."

"What?"

"You have this gift also, the sense of other's thinking. You don't use it. Now, back to the case?"

She, embarrassed but more curious than flustered, didn't care to chat about the case. She wanted to hear all about his mind-reading as well as his idea that she could read minds. She was impressed that he'd warned her about his seeing her fantasies before she went too far in them.

"Don't be impressed. It is difficult for me to see a fantasy like you have with me, a wonderful fantasy, when I cannot act on it. So I change the subject to the case. Okay?"

She took a long breath, shook her head and when she looked at him she could hear his thoughts. His mind said, "I waited for you." She finally spoke. "Why are you interested in my sister? Professionally?

"Professionally, I do not think I want to tell you so much. It is danger. But," he sipped his wine and popped an olive in his mouth, "you know why." He finished the sentence with the olive tucked to the side of his mouth for a second.

"I know why? What?"

"Who is the killer."

"What do you mean?"

"You know it. Think about it."

Barbara, astounded, mentally ran through as many Venetians as she could, even some Americans who lived there. *He had said "it."*

"I know 'it'?" she said.

"Is my English not correct? I mean plural."

"You mean, I know them. More than one?"

"*Si.*"

"*Si?*"

"*Si, yes, plural,*" he said then sipped his wine again, rolling another olive between his thumb and index finger.

When she saw his card on Louisa's bed table, she'd recognized the name immediately, but since the paper she had with Massimo's number on it didn't include a surname, she at first didn't make a connection. Any two Massimos could live in Venice. Later when she pulled the scrap of paper out of her coat pocket and saw the number he had given her, she decided to check the business card against it. It was the same Massimo, the medico legale.

"I am happy you phoned me. I was waiting."

This caused her to look square at him. *Is this what you meant before when I heard your mind say, "I waited for you," did you mean you were waiting for me to call? Or did you mean something more?*

More, she heard this mind say.

"Don't we have something nice to talk about, not the case? Like you, Barbara?" He took the olive, placed it near her lips as if offering it to her, a slight grin at the side of his mouth. As she looked down at the olive, he touched her lips with it, which parted them slowly. When she opened her mouth, he placed the olive gently on her tongue. His index finger then dropped tenderly over her bottom lip pulling it down slightly. The same finger, still less than an inch from her mouth, pointed at her for a second, his wrist slightly limp,

"*Tu sei simpatica* (You are nice). *E molto molto bella."* (and very very beautiful.) He pushed his glass further away from him and turned his entire body to face her at the bar where they were standing.

"Do not tell Louisa that my interest in her sister, you Barbara, is not professional."

Barbara couldn't think of one word, not in Italian or English, to say except "*Si.*" She whispered it as her gaze dropped to her hands clasped tightly in front of her. He too looked down at her clasped hands, around which he put his own. Then he slowly pulled them up to his mouth and gently kissed each of her fingers, while he held her hands still clasped. When he finished kissing her fingers, he raised his eyes to hers, saying nothing. Then, still holding her clasped hands, said something to the bartender in Venetian that sounded something like "in a moment" with a slight nod to their drinks and whispered at her, "Come ... with me."

She felt herself gliding out the door, he guiding her down a dark street as he shook his head up ahead towards the sea, "We go."

As they walked to the ocean, she relished the silence, his soft hand, his stride, her heat, the memory of those tiny kisses on every single finger. Abruptly she stopped and said, not at all sexy, but perky like a little girl at her birthday party, "Say something to me in Italian."

Amused, he asked, *"Cosa vuoi che dica?"* (What do you want me to say?) He continued to lead her towards the beach.

She, this time only slightly more seductive, still playful and excited, said, "Speak Italian to me, please."

He continued walking, more quickly, pulling her along further until he found a short brick wall outside a small park where he sat down, held both her hands in front of him, looked up at her and began speaking to her softly and romantically in Italian.

She didn't try to interpret, understand or care. She was mesmerized. She listened and breathed. Strongly. Forcefully. She closed her eyes and listened. It was poetry. An Italian poem. Something. It was Dante. She knew. As soon as she recognized it as Dante, he changed it.

"La domenica dopo pranzo presi una gondola a due remi e feci il giro dell'isola di Murano."

All that she understood were the phrases "in a gondola around Murano island" and Sunday after lunch." It didn't matter what the other words meant. It excited her. The sound of words, the thought of the two of them in a gondola. His voice. Everything. Everything about him.

Still reciting, he took his hands out of hers and placed his low around her waist, *"per perlustrare la riva del casino e scoprire la piccola porta del convento da cui usciva mia amica."*

Casanova? Was it something from Casanova? wondered Barbara.

Gently he pulled her down onto his lap, placed her hands around his neck, while he spoke Italian words she didn't know, the melody was enough. Then he stopped. She opened her eyes to see what he wanted, all he would say was *"Carina?"* (dear one). By this time she could barely breathe let alone speak, ready to push him back off the wall onto the ground, topple over him. But she managed to say, *"Cosa?"* (What?)

He repeated *"Carina,"* as if asking for something, this time his hips tilted slightly up towards hers and he stared directly at her lips and bit his own.

She understood what he wanted, and even if not, she did it anyway. She leaned down and kissed his bottom lip, the one he had bitten himself, then she kissed his top lip and lightly brushed her lips onto his. He didn't kiss back, this was his way of kissing back, to quietly receive hers lips on his. At first. Soon he was absolutely kissing back, deeply. At which point, she had to stop. It was all too much. The clothes must come off. Or she had to stop.

She put her hands under his chin and said, "The beach?"

"Mmmmm, okay the beach."

❧

"Cara," Barbara heard someone calling her "dear" in Italian, Louisa calling to her as she exited the dressing room in an eye-popping dress. It highlighted all of her curves, yet covered them completely.

"It's . . . amazing. Whatever the cost, buy it," said Barbara.

"Eight thousand euros."

"Maybe not." They both laughed at the thought of a dress costing over ten grand.

"Get ready to tell me everything. I can see in your dazed eyes, you were deep in boy-toy-land."

"No I wasn't," protested Barbara. *I was in heaven.*

"Yes you were-errrr," sang Louisa and entered the dressing room again to wishfully try on another perfectly crafted ensemble.

Barbara continued her musings about her evening with Massimo.

"To the beach," Barbara remembered Massimo saying to her. She had agreed, assured but as unsure as she had ever been. *What would they do at the beach? Sand, sand everywhere.*

"Don't worry," he leaned down and whispered.

They arrived at the beach, the moon hid partially behind a cloud. He pulled her to shore, stood behind her, pointed out to sea and said, "Ask yourself what is it you truly want, Barbara. Listen to the ocean sing to you, feel the wind. What is it? Do you know? If no, then ask and let it speak to you. What is it you want?"

She stood there feeling the power of the ocean before her and the lack of it in her heart. She had run from this moment all her life or so it seemed. He sensed it, pressed against her and, still from behind, wrapped both arms around her. First they stood silently then softly in her ear he said, "It's a good question, no?"

No kisses, no hands, simply an enchanting hug from behind, his firm chest on her back and warm arms enfolding her, his breath tickling on her neck, his legs running the length of hers. Massimo and the sight, sound and smell of the ocean surrounded her

"What is it you truly want, Barbara?"

❧

"Hello? Barbara?" Louisa was talking again. Barbara heard it and it jolted her out of her fantasy world. Louisa stood before her in another relentlessly sexy outfit.

Barbara tried to revive the vision of the ocean, to feel the presence of Massimo pressed against her from behind. The recreation failed her.

"Not as great?" Louisa said. "Still fantastic and only five thousand euro this time." She saw that Barbara wasn't listening and remained glassy-eyed in some fantasy state. "The dirt or not?" she said.

Louisa waited, almost as if she planned to hold her sister hostage to an ever-changing fashion show, flaunting her gorgeous physique and bottomless pocketbook until Barbara confessed.

"I wish I could tell you everything. Not here," said Barbara. They looked around to find three salesgirls and two Italian customers waiting to hear the dirt too.

"Let's go," clapped Louisa.

"Okay."

Barbara would have to tell gritty details of something to Louisa. Perhaps the Seba and Gianni escapade of her first night, adding some Venetian embellishment? She'd do anything to keep her mind and their conversation off of Massimo, whom she wanted all for herself and didn't want her more adventurous sister to get to know better.

Louisa's cell phone rang.

"Don't answer it," said Barbara. "Give me the phone."

"No," yelled Louisa as her sister grabbed it.

"Hello," Barbara said with a British accent.

"*Dai.*" (Come on.) Matteo's gruff voice said,

Eager to hear the sordid details of Barbara's threesome, Louisa lost interest in the search for clues from Venetian ghosts. Her obsession with Matteo faded. For now.

"Wrong number," Barbara said in bad fake Cockney when she saw Louisa signal for her to hang-up. Then she slapped the phone shut, plopped it into her bag and turned back to Louisa.

"Now, do you want to hear the dirt or not?"

BOOK CLUB QUESTIONS

1. Were you engaged immediately in the story or did it take you a while?
2. Describe the main characters—personality traits, motivations, inner qualities.
3. Is this a page-turner or does it unfold slowly with focus on character development? Were you surprised by the plot or was it predictable?
4. Does Diana use a single or shifting viewpoint? Why might Diana have chosen to tell the story the way she did—what difference does it make in the way you read or understand it?
5. What main ideas—themes—does Diana explore? (Consider the title, a clue to theme.) Does she use symbols to reinforce the main ideas?
6. What passages strike you as insightful or dialogue that is funny, poignant, encapsulates a character?
7. If you could ask Diana a question, what would you ask? Does this book inspire you to read her other books?
8. Has this novel changed you—broadened your perspective? Have you learned something new or been exposed to different ideas about people or a certain part of the world?
9. Who do you think sent Louisa the ghost letter?
10. Have you ever had a relationship with a guy like Matteo? If yes did you dump him, or marry him?
11. Have you ever had two men fight over you like Barbara did? If yes, what did you do?

12. Who do think Louisa looks like? Jennifer Aniston, Kristen Bell
13. Who do think Barbara looks like? Kim Kardasian, Kristen Stewart
14. Why do you think the Buranese snubbed Louisa?
15. Is Massimo a ghost? Explain.
16. Have you ever sensed the presence of a ghost? If yes, would like to blog about it? Haunted-palooza, in October, could publish you! Go to www.whathappensinvenice.com.

HAVE A VENETIAN GHOST PARTY!

Required Supplies

- Masks & Capes
- Gilded Things
- Red Velvet & Black Satin (to drape)
- Cobwebs, Mold, Candles or Gas Lamps
- Classical Music by Verdi, Vivaldi or Wagner
- Real & False Friends
- Merchants (to buy & sell stuff)
- Gondoliers (to provide many services)
- Murano Glassware
- Pigeons
- Bellinis (see recipe, www.whathappensinvenice.com)
- Cichetti (see recipe, Book Two, Lagoon Lure)

Additional/optional

- Loose Women & Eager Men

Millions of Wines, Millions of Cheeses

Pizza, Pasta, Pirates

COMING SOON!
What Happens in Venice: Book
Two *Lagoon Lure*
by DIANA CACHEY

༺❀༻

FANS

Shhhh . . . PEOPLE are talking about DIANA . . .

"Awesome, Diana. Interesting. It's simmering." Robert Allen, #1 New York Times Bestselling Author, over 72 millions copies sold.

༄༅

"I love your energy. You have a real talent. I think of you whenever anyone mentions Venice, which is often. I love this!!" Linda Sivertsen, BookMama & bestselling author

༄༅

"Diana is an engaging, witty and exceptional author writing a book about Venice. She will have you in love with the intrigue, romance, adventures and beauty of what goes on there in moments." Jen Todd, Author, CEO Breakthrough Partners

༄༅

More praise for What Happens In Venice:

Diana ROCKS! Grab on if you dare! And you too will find yourself floating. I promise!

WOW! Bravo. You really hit the essence of everyday life in Venice, combined with a first-timers viewpoint, great tips, romance and intrigue. From the very first page the reader is pulled in and captivated. Once again, BRAVO!

Love it!!!!!!!

The passion is dripping off your work, that is sooo very refreshing to see in among the noise out there.

Brava Bella Diana. I sit in awe. Baci Baci I want to read more!

Dear Diana, Wonderful, I await more.

Really wonderful! I can't wait to read more.

Thank you for your insight of your story. Sounds intriguing, motivating, happy! Good writing!!

Ciao Bella, Wow, this is impressive. Is it coming out on Kindle or in hard cover?

Your writing style alone intrigues. 'We prefer floating' is my favorite line.

I HEART your tale.

The excerpt sounds great, if the rest of the book is like it, you have an award winner or a bestseller in my opinion.

I read it this morning. It's a bestseller in the making.

AUTHOR BIOGRAPHY

Diana Cachey is a licensed attorney, published academic, and former adjunct law professor. She also holds a BA in English, and while in law school, she was the first female editor in chief of her university's law review.

The author of the novel *Love Spirits*, she has trained with several *New York Times* best-selling writers, including Robert Allen, with more than seventy-two million books sold.

For more than a decade, Cachey has been traveling to Venice, the setting of her novel, on extended trips several times a year. The cafés, restaurants, and many other haunts of Venice play a prominent role in her sexy paranormal mystery-romance about a beautiful American lawyer guided by the Ghosts of Venice in the investigation of a hushed-up crime.

Made in the USA
Lexington, KY
21 August 2014